AND *the*
SEAGRASS
FADES

---

to my friend, the reader:

AND *the* SEAGRASS FADES

KIAN SABIK

ALSO BY KIAN SABIK

The Huntdown Duology
Endangered
Abandoned

Standalones
Each Piece of Firewood

GLOSSARY

Akhi: Brother

Assalam Alaikum: Muslim greeting that means "peace be upon you"

Burqa: A long garment that covers head to toe

Dua: Prayer

In sha Allah: If God wills

Jahannam: Hell

Masjid: Mosque

Rabb: Lord

Shahadah: Islamic declaration of faith; highly recommended to repeat before death

Suqq: Market

Thawb: A shirt for men that goes down to the ankles

Walaikum Salam: Response to Assalam Alaikum

N
W
E
S
TURKEY
SYRIAN DEMOCRATIC FORCES
RAQQAH
ISLAMIC STATE
SYRIAN REGIME
DOUMA
DAMASCUS
SYRIAN REBELS
IRAQ
JORDAN
syria | 2018

PART I

yusuf

GUILT IS A thief. A thief of all joy, laughter, and comfort. It looms in every corner of your mind, flowing through your veins. It's like a splotch of blood, impossible to remove from your clothes. Even if you scrub and scrub at it, there are still hints of red. It's a reminder of the punishment you deserve.

Your sheet's frosty hands wrap themselves around you. They keep you in place, refusing to let go. Your joints are brittle and locked. The side of your neck aches from lying on the flat mattress for hours. Your fingers brush against the tense muscle but your hand drops down without a care.

You press your eyelids together, while your hand rests on the tile floor, numb from the cold. There's only a slight tingle in your feet that alerts you to their presence.

Tap. Tap.

You shift a little. Your eyes trace the wooden swirls on the shut door. They almost rattle when the knocks come. "Yusuf? I have dinner," your aunt's muffled voice peeps.

You try to open your mouth but it's thick and crusty. Your throat is arid, only scratchy breaths climbing out.

Tap. Tap.

"Yusuf?"

A sigh erupts from your lungs. The familiar song of the wall pulls you back toward it and you gaze at the carved shapes in front of you. A couple of lines to your left form a car, its tires barely visible in the shadows. To your right is a deformed shoe, its laces spilling to the side.

You inch forward until the skin on your forehead folds against the objects drawn into the wall. You rub your head up and down until you feel the prick of wood piercing your skin.

Something hard pinches the inside of your arm. Your eyes flicker down, toward the red dinosaur biting into your flesh. Its head fades into the black of your shirt, as if hiding in shame. On its back, one of its spikes is creased along the middle, the top half leaning toward the left. You carefully position the top into place but it still sticks out just a bit. Your hand falls a bit to caress its scales.

A drop streams down your face. You bring the toy toward you, hugging it despite the barbs digging into the gaps between your ribs. The drop falls onto your sleeve and it clings to your skin. You pull your blanket over yourself, muffling the sob stuck in your throat.

laila

DESPAIR IS THE ocean. The water's icy fingers wrap around a sailor's ankles, pulling him deeper into the endless black. Death knocks on his lungs, watching as the desperate bubbles climb to the distant surface. An eerie silence begins to settle in his ears and that's when he knows it's over.

Or it's like the sky, its eyes trailing everywhere. No matter how hard its victim tries to hide, they can never escape the sky…unless they're dead. But even then, it will haunt them, filling their heart with the dread of never seeing light again, even though they were trying to outrun it just seconds earlier.

I shield my eyes from the pesky ray of sunlight poking them. The burning patch of skin now feels like ice, missing the heat. I massage my tense ankles, ears perking up as soft footsteps hit the dirt.

"Found you," a shrill voice rings.

My stomach knots itself as I lean toward the gap between the barrels I'm squatting behind. My hand drops and the ray of sunlight returns with full force.

From the little space between the barrels, I can make out a child's back. They're arched forward, their face cut off by a wall. One of their arms is outstretched above them, as if resting on a wall. My eyes drift to the side, landing on the brown and gray everywhere. The ground, the houses, the buildings, all of it looks the same.

Everything is dull.

Just like the minutes. All of my days are the same, tedious jumble. There's nothing to look forward to. Nothing to look behind at. Nothing to look toward at all. There's no point in having fun or making memories. All around me are constant reminders of the life we barely live. Even this meager game is a reminder of the piles of bombed walls, leftover guns, and tattered shirts.

"Now we just have to find three more people and we win," the same shrill voice chirps.

I shift my feet a little. A thin shadow lands in front of the gap. I look up ever so slightly to see a young boy with jagged, black hair. "There's no one here," he declares, "Let's go check the trash cans behind the neighboring houses. There are usually a lot of people hiding there."

The voices retreat, along with their footsteps. I lean against a wall behind me, a sudden rush of blood soaring through my feet. The ray of sun stings my skin with renewed determination.

My bones beg for relief from squatting. I scan the deserted street, stretching my eyes as far to the side as possible. My ears strain to hear anything other than the humid breeze disturbing the dust. A bead of sweat drips down my neck and the air around me grows thick and hot.

I tip forward until my head is completely outside the protection of the barrels. The air is more free and pulls me out into the open. My knees shriek in protest, forcing me to stand bent toward my left. I take a step forward, my torn shoes scraping the pebbles on the street.

"I hear something," a girl yells and a thunder of footprints storms toward me. A spike of adrenaline rushes through my veins. My legs propel forward, pulling me into the shaded abyss of an alley. I glance over my shoulder right before tumbling over a barbed chunk of wall. A cloud of dust climbs up my nose and I slap a hand over my mouth to muffle a cough.

I grip the edge of the pile and dare to peek. Several feet away, a girl peers into the opening of the alley, her toes drawing in the dirt nervously.

"Go check if anyone's there," the jagged hair boy commands.

The girl shakes her head, her light brown curls whipping her face.

"Why not? Are you scared?" the boy teases.

"No, I just don't want to," she huffs.

"Fine, go look somewhere else." He enters the alley, his breathing heavy.

"Is anyone here?" he calls out. My heart begins to hammer against my ribs as his footsteps ring in my ears.

And then they stop. I push myself against the wall beside me, my face tingling as it touches the cool surface. I squeeze my eyes shut while the boy shuffles.

Thud.

I stifle a yelp, flinching hard against the brick wall. The rock the boy threw rolls toward my feet.

"I don't think anyone's in there," the girl peeps, "Someone would have screamed after you threw that rock."

"I guess," the jagged hair boy mutters. A couple seconds later, the crunching of dirt drifts into the distance. I crack open my eyes and blink rapidly, the black void around me morphing into shades of gray and brown. My throat relaxes, allowing air to flow through. I peel myself off the wall and let my head roll to the side.

My eyes latch onto the silhouette of a figure in the far end of the dark alley. Their head is between their knees while their thick hair dangles in front of their pale neck.

I cock my head to the side, straining to get a clear image of the figure. My eyes trace their limbs until they land on their clenched hands. A blue Superman bandage peels off the corner of their finger.

"Amir," I whisper. The figure doesn't stir. I peer over the debris pile, making sure no one is out there. *"Amir."*

Amir raises his head, a shadow eating his face. The only thing visible are his eyes. I tilt my head a bit to the left and suddenly my vision is shrouded in the lush green of his irises.

"We should get out of here," Amir starts, "They'll check the alley again once they realize we're still hiding." His last words are muffled by a yawn.

"Did you not sleep last night?" My voice is just a faint sound in the breeze.

He shakes his head vigorously right before crawling toward me. He plops down to the ground, resting his head on my shoulder. A smile tugs on the corners of my mouth. I rest my hand on his arm, rubbing it back and forth.

I tilt my head backward toward the line where the sky meets the brick wall. From the rooftop, a stream of dust trickles down, collecting in a pile inches from my feet. The mound rises and falls with more dust, syncing with Amir's gentle breathing.

One-hundred-six,
one-hundred-seven,
one-hundred-eight,
one-hundred-nine.

Amir tenses a bit, right before lifting his head from my shoulder. He pulls his arms over his head while a grunt escapes his lips. "I can't fall asleep in the middle of hide-and-seek. What if I start snoring?"

Amir gapes as another yawn breaks out. "I need to keep moving."

"I'll come too." My knees pop as I extend them.

We step out from behind the rubble. I search the streets. Light gushes toward us, wrapping us in its blinding blanket. But it's just a disguise, a mirage, an apology for the overwhelming heat that threatens to detonate at any second.

"Gotcha," a voice bursts in my ear. I jerk toward the sound, my hands clapping over my ears.

A *BOOM* rings in my ears. I shake my head. *No, no, no. It's not real. It's not real. There's no bomb here. It's just a kid. Just a kid.*

I crouch down, digging my nails into the tips of my fingers. The air that was tight before loosens up, granting my lungs permission to breathe. Jagged Hair cocks his head a bit, his eyes locking onto mine.

"You thought you were so smart? Well, I outsmarted you," the Jagged Hair declares, a twinkle in his eyes.

I look up at his face. His forehead glints in the sunlight while his cheeks are flushed a bright, tomato red. Splotches of sweat and dirt coat his shirt, complimenting his ripped pants.

I reach out to ruffle his spiky hair with quivering fingers. My limbs are still tense from the *boom.*

Not a boom. A child.

Jagged Hair's laughter softens, along with the rest of his face. He gazes at my hand while heaviness replaces the twinkle in his eyes. He leans forward until the top of his head touches my hand.

After a couple seconds, Jagged Hair breaks away, a slight bounce to his walk. He cups his hands over his mouth. "I found another one."

Footsteps echo from behind me. I twist my head to see a few more kids gathering around the two of us.

Jagged Hair jumps up and down. "I found a big kid," he bursts. The other children look at him with awe. Jagged Hair raises a fist into the air.

"Now, two more people and then we win."

The children begin to cheer and I watch the twinkle in their eyes. Each one has a distinct glimmer, a unique hope.

I dig my nails deeper into my flesh. I used to have that glimmer too. I was just as innocent and clueless as they are. I was just as happy as they are.

But that's the thing: I *was.*

And no matter how hard I try now, I've realized there's no point to any of it, none at all.

I shove the thought away. "So I'm a seeker now?" I whisper.

A girl from the group nods. She grips onto a stick and begins to hike up the street. The children band into a circle, huddling and whispering. They glance up at me sometimes but return back to the conversation within a split second.

I turn so that the sun is eating my back. My cheeks are burning and when I bring my hand up to touch them, it's as if the skin has melted right off my face. A light, humid breeze ruffles my hijab. Clouds of dust twirl in the brief respite but after a couple seconds, their dance fades away.

I turn back but the group of kids have vanished, their faint laughter the only sign that they were there in the first place. I walk up the street, the houses beside me flying. Sand scuffs my feet, rubbing through the tears in the soles of my tennis shoes.

Up ahead, the street breaks into the outskirts of Douma. Tracks of brown-yellow land surround our town, as if protecting it from other cities. If I squint hard enough, I can make out speckles of green cultivated by the few farmers that are still alive.

A sharp pain erupts from my feet. I lift them up and run my fingers along the dry, red cuts along my skin.

A shadow inches toward my heels, offering the tiniest bit of refuge from the sun. My neck begs to look up, to search for signs of rain.

But my mind says otherwise. There's no point in looking up. There's no hope for rain. There hasn't been any sign of rain for weeks.

I close my eyes. *But maybe, just maybe there's a chance.* I cautiously glance upward. It's just a single, thin cloud attempting to veil the town from the sun. It isn't painted with a single hint of gray; it's an empty, taunting white.

My head drops back to the ground as I suck in a sharp breath. I clench my hands into fists. My heart begs for forgiveness.

The sky is merciless. I already knew that. So why, why, why would I look up? Why would I allow myself to have even a seed of hope? It's better to have no hope than false hope. No hope means less pain. No hope means knowing the truth of reality.

I focus on the individual stones in the ground. My eyes trail the cracks in the dirt and it's as if I can see the cracks on my own tongue.

I lick my lips and swallow a clump of saliva but it offers no relief.

It never has.

samira

GRIEF IS A suitcase that is my only company down the lonely, foggy road ahead of me. The handle is slick with sweat while my arm is stiff from the constant hauling. The back of my legs tingle as the suitcase slams against them again,

And again,

And again.

The bag rattles as I roll it over the pebbles on the street. With every tremble, sparks of terror rush through my veins and my mind jerks back to the priceless memories inside. But when my hand hovers over the zipper, I freeze. My fingertips quiver.

As soon as I pull the zipper, I know there's no turning back at that point. It's impossible to shed grief once it's sunk its teeth into flesh just like it's impossible to stop a lion from the hunt.

I rest my head against a wall, fingers trailing a crack. My arm outstretches in front of me until the crack runs away, laughing at my meager attempt. It ducks behind the bedroom door and I can almost hear it still laughing. It's almost as if it's taunting me to come find it.

I shove my feet into a blanket. At first, the icy cloth bites into my skin but after digging my feet deeper, heat begins to prick my flesh. Beside me, a sea of maroon bedsheets rises and falls. It compliments the gray pillow, which dips in the middle from years of use. Now, it barely protects me from the bumps on the wall.

I shift a bit, feeling myself lean toward the right. The bed *creaks,* straining from the pressure. But I've never had the energy to fix it.

I heave my legs over the side of the bed and pull myself up. My muscles are tight, forcing my body to curl inward. I step out into the dimly lit hallway and press my ear against Yusuf's door. The hot wood sears my skin.

It's complete utter silence, as if the dead live on the other side. I sigh and walk down the dusty hallway. Along the walls are a couple of frames, each one holding a treasured memory. I stop in front of one.

"Which one is my ring finger?" Zayd asks.

I rub my chin. Zayd grins, closing his eyes in mockery. His teeth sparkle in the sun. My finger hovers over his puzzle of fingers. I pull one.

"This one."

His fingers undo themselves and my nail is touching the tip of his thumb. My jaw drops. "Not possible," I pout.

Zayd sticks his tongue out. "No one can outsmart Zayd the Magician."

I bite my lips and tilt my head backward as soon as water pricks my eyes. I blink rapidly.

I have to be there for Yusuf. I have to be the emotionally stable one. I can't have him hear me cry.

I step out of the dark hallway into the living room. It's airy and light with hints of heat floating toward the ceiling. A gray sofa rests along a wall, its edges faded over the years. A couple of orange, white, and black pillows with thick layers of dust are thrown along the back.

To the left of the living room is a narrow entrance to the kitchen. I wrap my fingers against the thin wall and peer inside. There are a couple of light wooden cabinets hanging above the white marble counters. The cabinet door that shields the tiny fridge is wide open. I walk toward it, running my hand against the wooden knife block, the pans, and the stovetop. My arm drops a little, my fingers hooking onto the cabinet handle and shutting it closed.

"Krrrra." I turn toward the sharp cry, my gaze landing on a large, green parrot. Its eyes are like the night sky, deep and mysterious. But there's the hint of stars that circle its eyes, just like there are streaks of light blue sky on its wings.

"Krrrra," Couscous calls again. I walk toward the end of the kitchen toward a window and reach inside the cage to pet its cloud feathers. It purrs, rubbing its body against my hand.

I rest my head on my hand as I glance outside the window, one hand still stroking Couscous' chin. The world is painted red and orange by the sun's soft rays. An apartment building blocks the sinking ball of flame from my eyes. A couple of thick vines rush up the building, trying to mend the cracks. To the sides are some houses, half the size of the building. They're painted different shades of brick-red, gray, and brown. The burnt, naked trees almost perfectly blend into them.

From the gaps between the houses, I can make out figures in green jumpsuits. Their faces are shielded by black turbans wrapped around. On their shoulders rest rifles that stick out like extensions to their bodies.

A gentle *thud* resonates throughout the kitchen. I whip backward, ears perked up. But the sound doesn't ring again.

I travel through the apartment until I'm in front of Yusuf's room.

Tap. Tap. Tap.

"Yusuf?" I hear my voice echo inside his room. Complete silence.

I rest my forehead on the door. A bead of sweat drips down my face, catching the last glimpses of sunlight.

"Come out to eat."

Something stirs inside and I step out of the entrance. Yusuf emerges, wearing the same faded jeans and torn, green shirt from last week. From between the holes in his clothes, patches of uneven, brown skin peek out. A strong, musty odor slaps my face and I control the impulse to cup my nose. Yusuf freezes in the doorway. Strands of overgrown, black hair hang over his bloodshot eyes and highlight the deep, hollow circles sagging to his cheeks.

I step back and flicker my eyes toward the floor. But when he doesn't move, I glance upward. His unfocused pupils barely keep on mine. I point toward the kitchen. He looks at my hand and then the table and then back at my hand.

After a couple of seconds, he trudges toward the table, his feet scuffing the floor. I inhale deeply.

He pauses as I do, only continuing once I've fully exhaled.

I fiddle with my fingers, weaving them together. A smile tugs at my lips. One more day, one more meal.

I snap back into reality. The kitchen cabinets, walls, and table before me grows crisp and so does the figure staring at the chair. A halo of light circles his thin frame, as if highlighting his gray.

I drag myself toward him and pull out a chair, gently pushing him down to sit. Yusuf obeys but his head still hangs, limp. I tear a loaf of bread into four parts and spread a penny-worth of hummus on each.

I lay one in front of Yusuf. His foggy eyes flicker toward it. He presses his torn lips together for a split second before they fall open once again.

yusuf

THE ICY WOOD of the chair scrapes against your back. Your feet are tangled among themselves, a gentle spot of warmth spreading in your toes. But as soon as you move, the warmth turns into snow.

You stare blankly at the plate in front of you, at the slice of bread glaring right back at you. Spots of white peek from beneath the brown-orange hummus. In your lap, your fingers point toward the food. Your stomach purrs.

But you don't move.

You can't move.

Your arms are weighed down and your stomach ties itself into a maze of knots. A clump climbs up your throat.

You reach out and push the plate to the other side of the table. Aunt Samira's eyes dart from the dish to you. She opens her mouth as soon as her gaze lands on you but she hesitates.

You tear yourself off the chair and trudge toward your room. The heavy door *creaks* open and a gust of stale air carries a stench. The second you step in, a sizzling smell hits you.

Click.

The door shuts behind you and you take four wobbly steps before shattering onto your mattress. A patch of watery light gathers in the corner of the wall, the only sign of the sun through the black curtains. Through the thin foam of the mattress, you can feel the rocky, boiling tiles along your back.

A pair of slippers rest a couple of inches from your feet. The soles are faded from the sides while a layer of dust sleeps on the top. It's as if they're melting into the ground.

Tap. Tap.

The familiar knocks on the door ring in your ears but you shut them out, draping your arm over your head.

"Yusuf? Can I come in?" Aunt Samira calls out.

Silence.

"I've brought your dinner."

You grimace. The door whines open and a sliver of unwelcome light stings your shut eyelids. Gentle footsteps creep toward you.

"Here's your food," Aunt says. You open your mouth but your words are sticky and clumpy in your throat.

"Let me put it this way. You need to eat. Otherwise, you'll die. When I come back, this plate should be empty." She exhales and her voice cracks. "Please?"

The last word is so meek, it tickles your ear. Seconds later, the light from the door vanishes and you're left alone again.

You turn away from the wall and glance down. A couple of crumbs are scattered across the plate. You reach out to collect them, running your finger against the deep crack on the white clay.

You kick your blanket to the side and lean on your arm. The bread is cut in half by a stray strand of your hair. Your stomach catches sight of the bread again and begins to plead. With heavy hands, you reach for it. But as soon as your finger touches the crust, you recoil and your stomach lurches toward your throat.

You pull your blanket over your face and shut your eyes.

laila

I PEER OVER a barrel to find a girl crouched behind it. Her hands are in her hair, struggling to pull the knots out. She throws a finger over her lips, her eyes sparkling as they beg.

I muster a smile. "Found you."

"You can pretend you never saw me," she whispers, cupping a hand over one side of her mouth.

I shake my head. She sticks out her lower lip and pulls herself off the ground. When her wiry limbs extend, her skin barely hangs on to her bones. Her feet are exposed, painted with purple and red. "Where should I look, *boss?*" she asks, sticking her tongue out at the end of the sentence.

I shrug. She sighs and kicks a pebble near her feet. "I'll go check behind the houses then," she says.

I nod. She raises her hand to a salute and then darts into the looming shadows of the alleys to the right. I run my hand against the top of a shard of debris, my fingers leaving a trail in the thin, brown layer.

I rub my fingers together, watching as the dust scatters in the air.

A scream pierces the air. It's sharp and heart-wrenching, electrocuting my blood.

Another one. My fingers wrap around the debris. My heart begins to race.

Thump.

Thump.

Thump.

Then, *BANG.*

Utter, infinite silence. The faint footsteps, the gentle laughter, the waning wind, all of it is dead with a single gunshot.

My chest twists, the muscles contracting so hard, no air is able to enter. My legs turn into the ocean, sloshing until they can't hold it anymore.

Boom.

I squeeze my head. No, no. It's not that. It's not. It was a gunshot, not that.

But my mind refuses to listen. Blood surges through my limbs, threatening to burst out of my veins. I dig my nails into my hijab, twisting the cloth.

It's not that. It's not that. It's not *that.*

Amir.

Amir.

I crack open my eyes, forcing them to dart right and left. "Amir," I shriek. I spring off the floor. *"Amir. Amir."*

Soft footsteps creep toward me. I whip backward. *"No-"* I start but a hand clamps onto my mouth. Amir's terrified eyes lower to mine. His finger stands upright in front of his lips.

"Let's go," he whispers, peeling his sticky hand off my face. He grips onto my wrist and pulls the two of us beside an apartment building and into the alleys.

"Inside," he whispers. His hand tugs on mine and we retreat deeper into the shadows. Amir glues himself to a wall, sliding across the smooth surface. He peeks behind a sharp corner before gesturing me forward.

The second he disappears behind the bend, my heart picks up. Something creeps up behind me. I whip backward, eyes catching the white plastic bag tumbling on the ground.

I'm paranoid. There's nothing here. We're safe. We're safe.

No, you're not. A voice booms from the depths of my mind. *You're lying to yourself. You're just as exposed here. The alley can't protect you from anything. In fact, you're trapped. There's nowhere to hide.*

"I'm safe. I'm safe. I'm safe," I chant.

Creeeeak.

A chill runs down my spine and I squeeze my eyes shut. "I'm safe. I'm safe. I'm safe."

I turn a corner and something slams into my head. I take a cautious step back, rubbing my forehead while my vision focuses on the jagged wood fence in front of me. Amir's eyes dart side-to-side, right before he curls his fingers on top of the fence and pulls himself over. I reach out to rest my hand on the fence.

Bang. Bang. Bang.

I jerk backward, spinning toward the sound. But it's everywhere. Right. Left. Up. Down. Inside. Outside.

Everywhere.

I stagger toward the fence, forcing myself to grip onto the sharp wood. My fingers quiver against the planks, the vibrating ringing in my ears.

"Hurry up," Amir whispers sharply from the other side.

I grunt as I tug myself over the fence. My knees buckle as I land on the other side, my face slamming into the dirt. I throw myself off the floor and dash toward the back door. But my neck is wrenched backward. The air in my throat gushes out of me as the force grows tighter and tighter.

And then it lets go. The muscles in my neck relax as something slips down my back. Amir steps from behind me, his fingers wrapping the loose ends of my hijab over my shoulders. I glance down at them and reach up to rub the frayed, faded threads between my fingers.

"It was stuck," Amir mutters before turning the doorknob. "Get the ceiling," I order, rushing into the house. I pull the curtains over the two windows, watching as the squares of white light fade into darkness. I check the front door, rattling the doorknob to make sure it's locked.

Something flops behind me. I jerk, watching Amir tie the flailing end of the cloth "roof" onto a sharp piece of the ceiling. Soon, the house is plunged into total gray.

I collapse onto a mattress in the corner of the house. The sheet crumples as Amir curls in beside me, resting his head on my shoulder. His hair bounces up and down with my thundering pulse.

Bang.

I jolt, my ears bursting with the sound of the gunshot. Amir squeezes my hand. "It'll be over soon. We just have to wait, just like we always do," he murmurs.

samira

"YUSUF?" I CALL TO the lump on the floor. His thin blanket lays over him like he's resting in his coffin. It reveals the shapes of his bones, the sharp turns of his shoulders and his bare ribcage. His skin is gray and ragged, as if he's been poisoned. I crouch down next to him

I glance toward the untouched plate "Yusuf, you haven't eaten."

He doesn't respond, keeping his eyes shut. My fingers tap his shoulder. "Yusuf, you need to eat."

No response. I pull on his arm, dragging his body upward. His glassy eyes land on the plate in front of him. I tuck one of his wild curls behind his ear, right before holding the bread to his mouth. His lips part ever so slightly.

Bite by bite, I inch the bread into his mouth until it's all gone. I smile at him but it's not returned, just like every other time. Right before he lies back down, Yusuf's eyes flicker toward me. His fingers reach for his blanket, pulling the tattered cloth over him. I yank it off.

"It's the middle of summer. Why are you using a blanket?"

He turns toward the wall, pulling his legs up to his chest. As my fingers work the blanket, my eyes trace the loose threads spraying from the corners. I rub it between my fingers, watching as another tear cracks open.

"I'll be right back," I announce. I step across the hall into my room. I crouch to look under my bed. Zayd's blanket should be down here somewhere. Toward the far end is an orange pile. I reach for it, my fingers wrapping around the furry blanket.

I saunter into Yusuf's room, dropping the folded mass near his feet. "If it gets cold at night, use it but otherwise, don't. You'll overheat."

I don't get a response but what did I expect? Nothing really. The boy is barely alive and he blames himself for everything that happened.

I crack open the door when gentle, rhythmic sounds echo from behind me. I glance over my shoulder to see Yusuf gently patting his arm.

My heart lurches. My hand drops from the doorknob and I make my way back to Yusuf's bedside. I swat his hand away from his arm, taking over and soon, Yusuf's shoulders relax.

A soft hum forms in my throat. A melody that my parents sang when I was a child. A song that would play in my dreams for years afterward. My throat begins to vibrate with the familiar notes.

But as soon as they do, Yusuf stiffens. He shoots straight up, his eyes wide. He shakes his head rapidly. "Baba," he croaks.

I forgot. I completely forgot my brother used to hum that to his kids as well. I forgot Yusuf would remember. A lump forms in my throat.

Yusuf is still staring at me with heavy eyes. I open my dry mouth. "I'm sorry. I'm so sorry. I didn't mean to," I whisper.

He nods ever so slightly and lays back down. My chest tightens. What was I thinking? Why would I remind him of his family again? Why do I have to be so stupid? Why can't I take care of him properly?

How did I expect to be a mother when I can't even do this right?

.   .   .

I tickle Couscous under his chin and he purrs. A slight smile tugs on my lips but it falls almost instantly when Yusuf grunts in his room. I can't help thinking about my blunder. I reminded him of why he's like this. He beats himself over the accident everyday and yet I still reminded him of what he lost.

I lean onto the windowsill, wrapping my head in my arms. The darkness offers a bit of solace from the day's sorrow.

Couscous clicks his beak, his head cocked to the side. I reach into the bag on the floor and toss a couple of seeds into the cage, my eyes fixed on the world outside.

Streaks of black infect Raqqa's sky, a hint of white dots peeking behind the apartment building. Businessmen close up their shops, slipping their keys into their holes. Some workers wander the streets a bit, chuckling with their friends. Curtains are pulled closed, shielding the children and women they hold from the dangers of the world. The breeze is stronger now, streams of dust floating with a new energy. Beyond the houses, the sun peeks from behind a distant hill, just a sliver of its beauty remaining.

As the minutes pass by, the landscape grows quieter and quieter. The birds begin to hush, letting the crickets take over with their soothing song. A soft blanket inches over the Earth, black swallowing the final traces of light.

And as soon as it's pitch black, something glints in the darkness. Minutes later, the sky is dotted with specks of white and yellow. I trace my finger along the stars. A bear charges into a turtle. A fish flashes its diamond scales beneath a wave. And then, a house.

Zayd rubs my shoulders, warmth spreading through my arms. The light from the candle catches on his ring, the silver smiling at me. My eyes drift to the ring on my finger. It's thin and simple, a band of gold. I swipe at it.

"Look," Zayd whispers, tilting my head back so I can look through the top half of the window. His finger draws out a house. "One day, I'll buy you a house. We'll have three rooms. One for us, one for our son and one for our daughter."

"How do you know we'll have a son and a daughter?"

He shrugs. "Maybe we'll have two sons or two daughters. Maybe we'll have one daughter or one son. It doesn't matter. As long as you're happy and our home is filled with laughter."

"Babies cry a lot so you won't have your home of laughter for a while," I chuckle.

"But eventually, it'll turn into laughter. Beautiful things take time but the wait is the best part. The anticipation, the hope, that's what keeps everyone alive. That's what makes us, us. Our desire to see our wishes come true. Our desire to one day touch the stars and not be afraid of the emptiness beneath us."

Zayd smiles and wraps an arm around my shoulder.

yusuf

FROM THE WORLD beyond your door, not a single sound drifts toward your ears. Your foot twitches, a gentle *clang* echoing from the wall. It's the only sign that you're *still* alive.

The shallow sleep you were in has floated away. Your finger can almost touch it, almost, but almost isn't enough. It's never enough.

You rub the dinosaur between its spikes, your nail catching on the bumps along its skin. It gapes at you, pupils dilated in fear. It's as if it was frozen alive in its last moments, when it realized it would never experience the warmth of life again.

You rest the toy on your hand.

"Mama. Mama. Look at this." Mahmoud gallops toward you and your mother, his hands delicately wrapped around a toy. His chest rises and falls. *"Can we buy it?"*

Mama reaches for the toy. It's a small, red dinosaur, no taller than four inches. Spikes shroud its back and tails while its mouth hangs open, as if it's calling out to something.

Mahmoud sticks out his lower lip as Mama's eyes examine the toy. "Please?" he whimpers.

Mama sighs but smiles. She turns toward the shopkeeper. "How much is this?"

The shopkeeper gazes at Mahmoud with a tender smile. A hint of sorrow is painted on his face. His words come out, hushed. "Two hundred liras."

Mama's smile breaks for just a second before her fingers dig into her pocket. Your eyes catch them rubbing the bills but eventually, she pulls them out. She glances at the papers, her lips moving as she counts, and hands four of them to the shopkeeper.

He bobs his head. "Thank you." He turns to Mahmoud. "Take care of it."

Mahmoud stares at the dinosaur in his hands, his eyes glimmering in the sunlight. He throws his arms up, right before leaping toward Mama and throws his hands around her legs. "Thank you, Mama. Thank you, thank you, thank you."

"Thank you."

"Thank you."

"Thank you."

You squeeze your eyes, trying to silence Mahmoud's voice.   But it settles in your ears, refusing to let you go.

A sharp, white pain radiates from your palm. You crack your eyes open to see the dinosaur's spikes biting your flesh, the skin around it streaked red and purple.

Your fingers brush your abdomen. Your skin tingles a bit, reminding you of the bursting organ inside. A quiver travels down your legs.

You have to go to the bathroom. You can't ignore it any longer.

You sigh, tearing yourself off the floor.

.   .   .

You collapse onto your bed as soon as your eyes settle on it. Your muscles ache from the dread of using the bathroom. You curl into yourself letting your vision adjust to the shadows around you. You glance back at the curtains, a blockade between you and the miserable, breathing world outside.

Your eyes flutter shut.

Boom. Boom.

laila

I REST MY head against the wall. Droplets of sweat drip down from my forehead and the thick air paints me with its gloss. The window is cracked open, just enough to let a soft gust of fresh air inside. It tickles my face just like it did then.

"Mama," I call from the other room.

"Yes?" she responds from the kitchen.

"Can you play with me?"

"Play with your brother," she responds from the kitchen. I rest my chin against the sofa and let my arms loose, watching as my hands bounce off each other again and again.

"I don't want to. I want to play with you."

Mama steps out into the living room, rubbing her hands on her shirt. It leaves a couple of dark streaks on the cloth. "I have to clean the kitchen right now and then put Amir to sleep."

I cross my arms. "You said after Amir was born, you'd still play with me. You only love him now."

Mama chuckles, glancing down at her watch. "Alright. Give me fifteen minutes to wrap this up and take care of Amir. Then I'll come. Deal?"

"Deal," I chirp.

.   .   .

"Baba will be back soon," I mutter.

Amir nods and reaches into one of two remaining cabinets. The wood pattern on each is distorted, almost burnt. The counter that remains is jagged, the edge a reminder of the attack a couple years ago. Rust bites into the grates on the dead stove. A candle rests on the counter, barely illuminating my surroundings. Amir reaches for the lightswitch but the gashes in the bulbs above refuse to respond.

"They won't turn on, you should know that by now," I grumble.

"You never know," Amir peeps.

I sigh and turn to the left. A red picnic blanket lies a couple of feet from where the wall was ripped off.

I set down three plates but my eyes remain on the side that's empty. The fabric there is untouched and flawless as if it's hoping for its guest.

But that's the thing. It's wrong for it to hope. It doesn't know that the person it's waiting for is trapped in a coffin.

Amir holds out his hand. "The glasses."

I nod and bend down to pluck them off the counter they were drying on hours ago. He trudges to the sink and cautiously fills each glass halfway from a jug. He sloshes the liquid inside. "This will only last for another day."

"Take some out from today's share. We can make it last two days," I mutter. My throat roars in protest but we have no choice.

Footsteps inch toward the front door and my ears perk up when the jangle of keys reaches them. My head snaps backward toward the door. Baba steps into the faint candlelight. An exhausted smile is plastered on his face, the wrinkles around his eyes burying his pupils. His short beard is tinged gray while freckles dot his sunburnt cheeks. His eyes remain fixed on the doorknob as he turns it shut.

I throw my arms around him. He buries his face into my neck, his beard tickling me. He opens his other arm and Amir squeezes between us. Baba plants a kiss on each of our foreheads, a gentle sigh escaping his lips.

"How was work?" I ask.

"Fine. The boss is a little worried he might go out of business. I heard him saying something about international business partners planning to back out. If that happens, his business won't have any customers since very few of us can afford computers."

Amir pulls away, resting a hand on Baba's shoulder. "Let's eat."

I grip onto Baba's briefcase, tugging it away from his fingers. His eyes jerk toward me, the terror in his eyes fading once he sees the bag cradled in my arms. "Oh, sorry...I'm still in that fight or flight mode."

"Hurry up, you guys. I'm hungry," Amir pouts.

Baba chuckles. "I'm coming, I'm coming."

He takes a step forward but I throw my arm in front of him. "Not so fast. You haven't washed your hands."

Baba turns to me with surprised eyes. "I go to work for one day and I've been taken over. It seems like you're the father now, young lady. Or should I say, Baba." He ruffles my hair.

"Hurry up, Baba," Amir whines. "I'm hungry. If you take a long time, I'll have to eat you."

Baba scoffs. "I'll eat you first."

Amir shakes his head. "I'm stronger than last time. All the running around from hide-and-seek has made my muscles grow."

"You'll never be stronger than your Baba, ever. Even if you manage to pin me down, you'll feel sorry for me and then," Baba swings over to Amir and tickles him, "I'll have the element of surprise."

"Stop, stop." Tears stream down Amir's face. I lay the briefcase on the floor and dive into the mess. My fingers hover over Amir's stomach.

"Not you too," he shrieks.

"Too late." I join in the tickling. His cheeks turn red and his raspy voice echoes throughout the house. "Stoooooop."

Baba steps away, rolling his sleeves up his forearm and wiping his sparkling forehead. "I'm going to get ready real quick and then we can eat."

"Hurry upppppp," Amir groans. Baba takes a baby step toward the bathroom across from the kitchen.

"I can go slower, if you'd like." Another baby step.

"Nooooo," Amir cries, a grin spreading across his face.

Baba takes an even smaller step, moving his foot two inches. Amir reaches for Baba's plate. "Hmm, it seems like no one has showed up for this plate yet. I guess I'll just *have* to eat it."

Baba shrugs. "Alright. I guess you can eat the plate if you're so hungry. Eat my glass too. I don't mind."

"I mean your bread," Amir cries.

"You never specified," Baba counters. Amir grunts and lies down on the ground, a bubble of laughter erupting from his throat. I chuckle, the sound echoing from my nose. Amir turns toward me. "I don't know why you control your laughter. Sometimes, I feel as if you're saving it up for something. As if you can only laugh once and then, never again."

"I don't do that."

"Yes you do."

"I don't."

"Whatever you say."

I weave my fingers together. Amir doesn't understand how hard it is to pretend. How I have to force myself to play with the neighborhood kids to avoid his questions. How I have to force myself to act happy in front of Baba so he doesn't worry. He doesn't understand that my laughter barely exists.

The bathroom door bursts open. Baba emerges, his hands glistening in the light. His collared shirt and tie are replaced by black pajama pants and a red shirt with the words "World's Greatest Dad." It's like a shirt on a hanger, puffed out to conceal the stick frame beneath it.

Baba's knees crack as he bends down to sit on the picnic blanket. He lowers his head, closing his eyes and whispering. "O Allah, bless this food and provide us with enough to meet our daily needs. Amen."

"Amen," Amir and I respond.

Baba lets the silence hang. "I can't wait any longer," Amir declares and shoves his bread into his mouth. He throws his head back, draining his cup. Baba and I look at each other, our eyes widened.

I reach for my food right before Amir burps, a hand rushing toward his lips. "Oops." He catches my eye. "What?"

"Disgusting," I mutter, glancing toward Baba, whose teeth sink into the hard piece in his hands.

samira

BOOM.

I shoot up. My eyes dart from side to side, catching on the orange glow in the distance. A stream of black, deeper than the night sky, climbs into the air. The stars' glow is shrouded by gray, another darkness settling over the city.

Boom.

My ears erupt with the sound and I slide onto the floor.

Clink. Thud. Crash.

The window rattles, its hinges whining. Dust floods to cover every inch of the glass, turning the black into brown. Panic squeezes my chest and a shooting pain sears through my left shoulder.

The orange outside distorts into swirls and the smoke turns into a hand, snatching the stars.

I shove my right hand into my pocket, fingers grazing the edge of my inhaler. I tug at it but something pulls it back. I twist and turn it until finally, it slips into my hand.

THUD.

My heart screams, my hand going limp. The inhaler clatters to the ground. I grab for my left shoulder, squeezing with the pain. The walls begin to close in.

One.

Two.

One.

Two.

The bomb could've been set off here. But it wasn't. It wasn't. We're alright. We're safe.

We're. Safe.

My heart begins to calm down, the drummer inside resting his arms. My throat cracks open, allowing air to soothe its walls.

My vision clears. I'm curled against the wall, my side hugging the concrete walls. Above me, Couscous' cage rattles and blurs of green slam into the metal bars.

"Shhh. Shhh," I croak but my voice is like the breeze, barely alive. I dig my palm into the tile floor, savoring the cold spreading through my hand.

"Yusuf. Yusuf," I whisper. I peel my eyes off the floor toward the silent hallway. He's fine. The silence from his room means he's fine. Everything's normal then.

A stream of dust sprays onto my head, the minuscule grains dripping onto the ground. I rub my face. The sky outside is still painted an ashy gray. The city is completely dead, robbed of all life and joy. Something catches the corner of my eyes. At the bottom right of the window, white cracks claw into the glass.

"No," I cry.

With the next bombing, the entire window will be destroyed. Dust and debris will flood into the house. I clutch my head.

I can't think about this right now. I need to focus on the present. What's happening right now. Not tomorrow, not yesterday, *right now.*

My ears ring. Behind me, gentle chuckles morph into voracious laughter. I cup my ears and let go, the voices still echoing throughout the room.

I tip-toe toward Yusuf's door and press my ear against the wall. It's deathly silent. I run my hand along the wall as I peek into the bathroom.

A light erupts in front of my face, forcing my hands to fly over my eyes. The laughter is now crisp in the air.

I blink rapidly. Two children stand on the counter. The boy looks about seven, his two front teeth missing. His brown hair is cut too short, barely touching his scalp. The girl is about five with hair as dark as night. Her thin fingers clutch a stuffed rabbit. Both of them stand on the edge of the sink with their eyes locked on a pile of towels on the ground.

The boy crouches and springs off, landing in the pile with a *flop*. A giggle erupts from his mouth. The girl stands there, her toes curled around the edge. She peers down.

"I'm scared," she whispers.

The boy smiles. "Come on. It's a small jump."

"But what if I fall?" the girl murmurs.

"I'll catch you."

The girl hesitates, swaying gently.

The boy holds his arms out. A lock of hair falls onto his face and he brushes it aside. He opens and closes his fingers, urging her forward.

The girl shakes her head, her lip quivering slightly. She peers over the edge again, her body tipping over the edge. Within a split second, her arms are flailing in the air as she tumbles off.

I lurch forward, my fingers brushing against the girl's arm. A shriek escapes my lips. The pile of cloth caves inward and two figures squirm. The girl blinks open her eyes, her pupils fixed on the arms hugging her torso.

The boy smiles. "See? I told you I would catch you."

A smile buds on my face and my stomach tingles. I step toward the children, my arms reaching to brush the hair away from their eyes, but they fade away. The white of the bathroom vanishes and it's pitch black again, the *whir* of pipes echoing throughout the room.

Something crawls down my cheek and I swat at it. My fingers come back wet.

I wrap my arms around myself, rubbing my sides. I can still remember my heart sinking when I realized I was falling off the sink. I still remember shielding my head, waiting for the *crack* of my bones slamming into the tiles. I still remember my brother's gentle smile when I dared to open my eyes.

I run my fingers across my face, wiping them on my shirt. The rough paint of the wall rubs against my back until I'm on the ground, resting my head on my knees. My mind whirs with memories. Memories of how my brother gave me his food when I wanted more because he was "full."

How he lulled me to sleep when my pet bird died. How he worked every night for a month to buy me Couscous.

How he stayed home after I begged him not to study in Turkey.

How he always knew when I was upset, even when my parents didn't.

How he always promised to be there.

How he did everything for me.

How he invited me to eat dinner every night with his family when Zayd was killed.

How he laughed right before the sickening *crash* echoed from the phone. How his soft, comforting voice whispered in my ears. "It's alright."

I rub my eyes against my knees, watching as a puddle forms on my dress. My skin burns with the contact and my head begins to pound. I allow myself to drift away, back to a time when there was peace.

yusuf

BOOM.

The ground trembles with the explosion, your teeth clattering against one another. You curl your fingers into the mattress.

You squeeze your eyes shut. Please let it be close. Let them bomb this area. Let this building fall to the ground, burying you inside.

But the gasps and the rustling in the kitchen tells you otherwise. It tells you that you are still safe. You strain to listen to the terror outside: people howling and houses folding.

If only it was you.

When your eyes jerk open, the light from the curtain is at its peak. You turn onto your back and trace the cracks on the walls until you reach the ceiling. It dips from the center as if a crater has formed on the floor above.

Tap. Tap.

Your eyes dart to the left. "Yusuf, can you come out?" Aunt calls.

You turn toward the wall.

"Yusuf? Yusuf, it's important. I know you don't want to get up but can you please come outside? Or can I come in?"

You sigh and close your eyes. "I'm coming in," she declares and two seconds later, her shadow looms over you.

"We don't have food," she says.

A stone lodges in your throat and no matter how hard you swallow, it doesn't budge.

"We have nothing to eat," she tries again.

You can't respond. Your lips are sewn together.

"Yusuf, please. I can't go. You know I can't. ISIS won't allow it. Zayd is dead and a woman without a husband isn't allowed outside. You're the only one who can go."

You remain frozen in place. Something cracks in her voice.

"Please, Yusuf," she pleads.

Guilt pinches your heart. Mama would have wanted you to do it. Mama wanted you to be a good person.

And now it's too late to be the son she wanted.

You toss your blanket aside and stand up. You keep your eyes focused on the floor and hold your hand out. You squeeze it open and shut.

Aunt steps back, her slippers sliding against the floor as she leaves the room. You lower your head further, letting your hair taint your vision.

From the kitchen, a drawer whines open and paper rustles against each other. Then, her slippers clammer back, one after the other. Dread clenches your throat until her feet are just a couple inches from yours.

.   .   .

The air outside is thick, laced with the smell of smoke and dust. The sunlight bites into your skin and sears your eyes. The houses around you begin to tremble in the heat. Some of them are cracked open, the intricate mess of wires, pipes and walls exposed to the world. A couple of sheets hang from as makeshift doors and you can make out figures resting in the shade. The few trees and bushes in the street are withered, the life flushed out of the now curled leaves.

The curled leaves that resemble the car that you destroyed. The lives that you stole.

Crash.

"Watch it," a soldier barks. The strap of his rifle catches on your arm. Your eyes remain fixed on his leather boots.

"Are you deaf?" The soldier growls. His words pierce your eardrums but your feet sink deeper in the ground. The soldier's hand flies across your face.

You barely feel it at all, only a slight tingle serving as a reminder. Your arm is bent at an unusual angle, your wrist now entangled in the strap.

"Looks like I'll have to do it myself," the soldier growls. Your arm is limp as he wrenches your wrist forward and tears his rifle from your grip.

When you blink, he's gone. The shopkeepers in the streets swarm toward their windows, the sunlight reflecting the fear in their eyes.

laila

THE CRICKETS' HARSH chirps give way to a stillness. The barren sticks of the bushes rustle in the breeze while the faint glow of moonlight peeks through the curtains, fighting with the yellow glow of the candle. I watch the flickering flame. It sways back and forth as Amir and Baba walk left and right. Amir rubs the cups with a few drops of water from the jug and leaves them on the picnic blanket to dry. Baba paces in circles, his eyes fixed on the tiny screen in his hands.

"What are you doing?" Amir asks.

I look up toward Amir's cocked head. His eyes are fixed on the phone in Baba's hand.

Baba lifts an eyebrow. "Hm?"

"What were you doing on the phone?"

Baba sighs. "They can't even leave me for a couple of hours. 'Work never ends,'" he mimics his boss in a squeaky voice.

Amir chuckles. I slip my fingers between the knots in the mattresses, letting them roll onto the floor. I set each one a couple of inches from the next, not too close but not too far. Amir jumps onto an air bubble bursting from the middle bed. It collapses as soon as he sits.

"Why can't it ever stay up?" he whines.

"The air can't hold you," I respond.

He pouts. "I know but I'm really light so it should be able to hold something."

Bzzz. Bzzz.

Baba's phone vibrates in his palm. He reaches for the front door. "I'll be right back. I have to attend this call. Get in bed."

The door *clicks* shut behind him. Amir looks at me from over his shoulder. "You heard the man. In bed."

Amir collapses, his arms and legs dramatically falling after him. "Do you think the ceiling will fall on us?"

I turn my head up, eyes following the deep cracks. "Probably."

Amir's voice is laced with fear. "What if it collapses when we're sleeping?"

"Then there's nothing we can do," I respond.

His head snaps toward me. "What do you mean? We can always do something about everything. You're no use. I'll ask Baba."

"He'll probably tell you the same thing." Or he'll lie to make you happy.

Amir huffs. The door cracks open and Baba steps inside. He runs a hand through his hair, letting a heavy breath out. He walks over to the counter and bends down to plug his phone into his portable battery. But right before he does, he turns to us. "You both haven't gone to sleep yet?" he asks.

"Baba, will the ceiling fall on us?" Amir chirps.

Baba's eyes flicker to the ceiling. "Well, those are deep cracks but I think it'll last for a while longer."

I bite my tongue. A lie, just like I predicted.

"How long is a while?" Amir asks.

"I don't know. But don't worry, it'll start creaking when it's about to collapse. When you hear that, run out the door. If we're sleeping, wake us up and we'll all leave."

"But then, where would we go?" Amir asks.

Baba's eyes crinkle. "We'll see then. There's no use in worrying about that right now." He bends down and kisses Amir's forehead and turns to do the same on mine. "I love you both," he whispers.

"I love you too," I respond.

.　　　.　　　.

My pulse rings in my ears as I turn to the right. Every so often, I can hear the muffled *bangs* from afar. Or I can hear the Earth tremble underneath my head with the *boom* of bombs. Sometimes, I can hear screaming and begging through the ground, the voices of those withering away, the whispers of their bones.

It's a constant reminder of the life we can never have.

I turn to face the ceiling, the heaviness in my eyes fading away. Through the sheet covering the ceiling, the soft glow of stars shines. I reach up, my fingertip covering one.

It's their fault too, along with the soldiers and President Assad. The stars stand there, far away from all the battles and massacres. They watch without saying a single word, even though they could if they tried. All they do is inspire the false hope of happiness to everyone and then, in the morning, they vanish, taking their broken promises with them. And then we realize, we've been abandoned, left for a country that wants to tear us apart.

Just like they tore Mama away from me.

"Mama, are you done?" I whine.

Mama holds a finger to her lips and gently returns the knob to its place. She wipes her hands on her apron. "Let's go."

I jump up and down. "Can we play hide-and-seek?"

She smiles. "Okay."

I clap my hands. "I want to be a seeker."

"Alright. Count to sixty and don't cheat. If I see you peeking, I'll come and eat you." She licks her lips.

"No," I shriek, "I'm not yummy."

"But you are, like a little chicken. I'll tickle you until you die and then cook you in a pot."

"I won't cheat. I won't."

She grins. "You'd better not. Now turn around and start counting."

I squeeze my eyes shut, listening to Mama's retreating footsteps.

I shake my head violently, trying to rattle the flashback out of my head.

"Fifty-eight, fifty-nine, sixty," I scream and dash out of the house. "I'm coming, Mamaaaaaaaaaaaaa."

I dash out the front door and into the street, the sun caresses my skin like the comfort of a blanket before I go to sleep. The neighborhood kids playing nearby become blurs in my vision.

I dive behind a couple of barrels, only to find the space empty. I peek into the side of our house, the fence door left wide open. The muffled sound of giggling echoes from inside. I tiptoe toward the end, eyes focused.

Suddenly, Mama springs out from a corner and I shriek, falling backward. When I open my eyes, Mama is laughing hysterically, air barely entering her lungs. Her face is red and her hand clenches her stomach.

"That's not fair. You can't scare people in hide-and-seek."

Her laughter softens. "And who said that?"

"It's in the rules. We have to do a rematch now."

"Alright, alright." Mama picks me off the floor. "But this is the last round."

I nod, run to the front door and clap my hands over my eyes. "One. Two. Three. Four. Five. Six..." When the word sixty *erupts from my throat, I run as far as my little legs can carry me. Clouds of dust bite at my heels. I climb the fence around our house, the alley growing clear. Something moves in the corner.*

"Ah-ha," I scream and shove my foot into a hole in the fence, pulling myself up until I can see the entire alley.

Footsteps storm from behind me. "Laila. Don't. Move," a horrified voice calls. My head snaps backward and my foot slips off the fence.

Kaboom.

samira

YUSUF GIVES A faint nod and shuts his room's door behind him. The money in my hands hangs like a weight on a pendulum, rocking my arms back and forth. I swing the cash onto the counter.

Heaviness pricks at the back of my eyes. It's not my fault. I can't leave the house. Ever since the extremist group ISIS conquered Raqqa, women have not been allowed outside without a male relative accompanying them. Now with everyone gone, I can't even step outside my own house without getting attacked.

I turn to face the window. The sun is bleeding onto the sky, streaks of red and orange running along the blue. A couple of sheer clouds dot the horizon, not a single sign of rain.

I sigh, dragging my feet across the tiled floor to my room. I crumple onto the bed, my body bouncing against the springs inside the mattress. No matter how hard I try to make Yusuf get out of the house, enjoy the sun, or savor food, all of the effort is wasted. He refuses to see the gift of life. Rather, it's a curse for him. A curse he's making himself live through.

So how can I help him?

I lean against my pillow, waiting for the answer to appear on the ceiling.

. . .

My fingers graze silk and I shoot straight up. Sitting in a plush, luxurious chair, Zayd has a book cracked on his legs. The moon illuminates the pages, the light glistening off his skin. His eyes move left and right as they scan the words. I glance down at the bed, balling up the cold, green sheets.

I try to throw my legs over the edge but they're glued to the mattress. "Zayd? Zayd?"

Zayd's eyes flicker up and land on me. He smiles gently, stretching as he does. He walks over to the bed and reaches out to...straighten the pillow behind me, a grunt escaping his lips as he examines the bed. "Zayd?" I peep.

He steps out the room, leaving the door slightly ajar.

"Zayd?" I call out, my voice stronger. But he doesn't return.

"Zayd," I shriek.

The door slams open. I jerk backward. My brother sprints into the room, hands flying around. "Where is it? Where is it?"

"Where is what?" I ask.

He reaches straight through my shoulder and lifts the pillow behind me. I shrink back, my heart hammering against my chest. He pulls out a wad of cash. "Oh, I found it."

My brother bounces with joy, right before closing the door behind him. I thrash against the bed but my wrists and ankles just pull on the mattress. "Zayd. Zayd. *Zayd.*"

No one comes. I glance down at my hands. My palm is still coated in brown skin but my fingers, the skin has been ripped off. The bleached, dead bones call out to me.

A scream rips from my throat.

yusuf

YOU KICK A pebble and watch it skid across the road. The dirt around it flies upward, disintegrating into the air. You step into the shade of a ledge, fingers turning the knob of the bakery. A heavy, floury smell slaps your nose and you recoil.

The baker's eyes dart toward you as he speaks to a child who's about ten years old. His hair is like the sand, with streaks of brown peeking from underneath. A wide gash runs across his chin.

When the baker puts up a finger toward me, the child's head snaps to his right. He nods slightly but his eyes are heavy.

"I'm sorry, I can't," the baker mutters, his head hanging low. The boy inhales sharply.

"Please. I don't have money. We're going to starve. My *mom* is going to starve," the boy cries.

The baker shakes his head. "My family needs the money too. I'm sorry."

The boy wipes his face, tears trickling from between his fingers. His voice comes out hushed. "Please."

The baker turns away and shakes his head.

"Please."

The baker looks up and gestures you forward. You step beside the boy. Two streams line his cheeks while red spreads in his eyes. He glances toward you. You keep your gaze forward, fixed on the baker.

Without a word, you hand him the money. The baker gives you three loaves and bobs his head. The boy is staring now, his mouth hanging open at the sight of the golden loaves in your hands. He opens his mouth but you turn and walk away.

laila

A TEAR DRIPS down my face. I grip the bulge on my hand, rubbing against what used to be my pinky.

My eyes flutter open, my eyelashes tickling the dust beneath me. I clench my throbbing head. Something warm brushes against my skin. I shift away from it, pressing against my hands until I'm sitting.

A dark lump appears to my left. I rub my eyes, the figure's outline growing clearer and clearer. A scream erupts from my throat.

"Mama. Mama. Mamaaaaa."

I shake her but her eyes remain cloudy.

"MAMAAAAAAAAAAAAAAAAAAAAA."

Sharp ringing echoes near my ears and I slap them but the buzzing continues unfazed. I sniffle, shaking Mama's shoulders. A fresh spot of blood appears. I glance down at my trembling hands, at the deep gash that's sliced my pinky in half.

Crystal tears begin to form a puddle beneath me. Everything around me begins to warp into brown blobs. I lace my fingers between Mama's icy, lifeless hands, rest my head on her arm and sob.

.   .   .

The sun peeks through the window when I shoot straight up. To my side, Amir's bed is barren, except for the crumpled sheet tossed to the side. Baba's mattress is rolled neatly in the corner. The shoes that occupied the mat only a few hours ago are gone.

The door to the bathroom swings open and Amir steps out, dark circles encompassing his eyes.

"Do you have anything planned for today?" he asks.

I shake my head. He casts his eyes down. "Can we go look for shoes?"

I glance down at his feet, barely lit by the dim glow from the window. One of his toes sticks out of a tear in his shoe while mud streaks every inch of them. The laces are frayed, stray threads baked into the dirt.

I nod. He sucks in a breath. "How about some clothes too?"

My eyes travel up, catching the inches of skin between Amir's ankles and his pants. The knees are so worn that they're almost see-through. His shirt hugs his boney torso, the sleeves clinging to his joints.

"Alright."

I nod and a sad smile spreads on his face. He moves toward a wooden chair near a window, its legs tipping forward as he does, slinging his arms back. "I'll wait for you to get ready then."

I close the door behind me and glance at the shard of mirror mounted on the wall. My eyes have sunken deep into my face, as if competing with my skin on who can collapse faster. A layer of dirt streaks my cheeks. I rub at it but it only spreads. My hair is a knotted mess, strands flying everywhere. I run my fingers through it but the tangles are stubborn, tearing my scalp.

I sigh. None of this really matters. It's not like I can avoid any of it. I tie my one black hijab over the bulge and step out of the bathroom. "That was fast," Amir remarks.

I shrug my shoulders. His eyes trail to the mass on my head and he furrows his eyebrows. "Is that your...hair?"

I nod. He cocks his head to the side. "Did you not comb it?"

"With what?"

He gestures toward his fingers. I stretch my mouth into a grimace. "Let me try," he says, stomping his feet on the ground in front of him.

I sit down on the floor and he unwraps the hijab. "That is one mess," he exclaims. I tense. "Sorry, sorry. I didn't mean to insult your hair."

He brushes a couple of strands off my face and then combs through my hair, untangling every strand.

I start to get up. "I don't think we have time for this."

Amir pulls on my hair so I fall right back down. "Shh. We have plenty of time. Now don't move."

"But—"

"*No buts young lady,*" he commands. "Be quiet so I can work my magic."

I lean against the wood and cross my arms in front of my chest. That child is as stubborn as a toddler. He'll tear my hair out of my head if I resist.

"Okay, all done," Amir declares after ten minutes, tying my hair. He stands and does a three-sixty. "What a masterpiece," he whispers.

I stare at him. "What?" he asks. "It really is. My hands turned that gigantic mess into something *presentable.*"

"Do you want me to break your feet into those shoes so that you never need another pair?"

He chuckles and shakes his head. "Let's go. It's first come, first serve, remember?"

.   .   .

We reach the outskirts of the city. The farmland is now the majority of the landscape, with a trench slithering between Douma and beyond. Near the deepest part of the trench lies a hill of junk, ranging from egg shells to car tires and everything in between. The thick air is laced with the smell of sewage and mold, the smell a slap to my nose. A couple of kids dot the pile, their hands searching through the scraps.

We stand near the base. My hand flies to cover my nose. Amir glances toward me. "You can't stay like that forever. Not when you're going to use both hands," he says. I turn toward him, watching his large eyes gaze at the pile of trash. His pupils are wide, with excitement bubbling out of them. If only I could be as hopeful as he is.

I sigh, letting my hand drop. I crinkle my nose as the smell taunts me further. Amir sits on his knees and reaches into the base of the pile. He pulls out a black shirt and examines it. "Too small?"

I nod and he tosses it to the side. A couple of kids scramble toward it, each one pulling a corner of the cloth.

"It's mine."

"I saw it first."

"I want it."

Amir climbs a step higher, throwing all the clothes he can get his hands on to the bottom. I pick a red one up and drop it. "This is still small."

The cycle continues for a couple more hours. The sun is now hidden behind the houses to our right. Exhaustion fills my muscles.

"Are we done?" I call out.

Amir thinks for a moment. "I think so. I can try them out at home."

He climbs down the pile and holds his arms out for the clothes. I dump them on him. Amir bends down to pick up a stick from the ground and holds it as we walk, drawing a thin track behind him. It jumps over pebbles, sparking the dust to life.

I speed up a bit, watching as the gray and brown homes become blurs in my vision. The occasional black holes of ripped walls gape at me, daring me to approach. A couple of cars are parked in front of some intact houses but even then, they are rusted and bruised.

Soon, I stop in front of our house. The black plastic sheet covering the ceiling flaps in the breeze. The curtain rod above the window in front of the kitchen hangs a bit from the right, a small gap in the blue cloth The metal knob on the door is dotted black, the sunlight glinting off of it and into my eyes.

Amir turns the doorknob, ushering me inside and takes off into the bathroom. Fabric rustles inside and then silence. It's as if I can see Amir examining himself in the mirror. A second later, he opens the door, revealing the loose green shirt and baggy jeans that hang from his skeleton frame. The gray shoes sheltering his feet are torn a bit from the top but the sole is rip-free.

"What do you think?" I ask.

He grins. "I think they'll last for a while. Maybe a year or so. Depends on how much I grow."

I nod. "Just hope that you don't grow too tall. Otherwise, we won't be able to find any clothes for you at all."

He taps his chin. "Well then, I might just have to wear the sheet I use to sleep. But if I'm tall, I'll be strong too. right? Then, I can protect you and Baba."

I freeze.

"I'm just joking. By then, we'll be out of here. Baba is saving for those airplane tickets, remember? In a couple of years, we'll be long gone from here." Amir closes the bathroom door behind him.

samira

CLICK.

The lock on the window snaps upward and I push the pane open. A gust of warm air tickles my face. A couple of stories down, the gentle murmur of passersby breaks the silence inside the apartment. Children gallop through the streets, weaving in and out of the light crowds. Some of the men yelp when they *whoosh* by but shake their heads with smiles on their faces and continue on.

A couple of women gaze out of their own windows, a mix of longing and fatigue in their heavy eyes. One of them catches my gaze and waves. I muster a weak one back and she resumes observing the throngs.

I smile at the children's beaming faces, the way their faces glow in the sunlight. How their half-extracted teeth shine through their grins.

I wish I had the bubbly presence of a child in my home. I wish Zayd could've come home to his child running to give him a hug. I wish we could've shown it the wonders of the sea, the changing weather, all the wonderful stories we knew.

But it's just wishes now.

A familiar figure enters from the left. Yusuf walks by the playing children, his head hanging toward the ground. His hair rests against his neck, licking his shoulders but he doesn't seem bothered. His feet drag against the ground, sending sparks of dust flying in the air. He doesn't smile, doesn't laugh, doesn't even look at anyone else. It's as if he's a shadow, forever gray.

Soon, he's past the window frame in a world I can't see. I reach out to touch the glass, praying for the day his cheerful self returns.

yusuf

YOU DRAG YOUR feet along the dirt. The black of the alleys followed by the brown and gray of buildings flash in your peripheral vision. It's the exact same scenery you passed earlier, only now you notice it less. The world has been so cruel to you so why should you care about it?

A hand shoots in front of you and you flinch hard. A man, whose face is masked with a black turban, glares at you from the slit between the cloth. He's dressed in green, crinkles near his wrists and ankles. A black belt sags on his waist, light glinting off the knives it holds. His hands grip on the rifle that rests on his shoulder.

"How old are you?" he barks. You stare at him and he snaps his fingers near your ears.

"Are you deaf? How old are you?"

You shrug your shoulders. The soldier stands up straighter, bringing his face close to yours.

"How. Old. Are. You?"

You flash ten and then eight with your fingers. He looks from your arms to your face. "Say it," he demands.

"Eighteen," you croak.

His eyes search you. "You're eighteen?" You nod slowly.

"You're required to join the ISIS army. Did you know that?"

You nod again. The soldier's eyes return to their narrowed position.

"You knew that but you *still* didn't join?"

You let your shoulders loose. A hand shakes your arm.

"You disobeyed orders?" The soldier's pupils are now unfocused, trembling with every movement.

"You disobeyed orders?" A hot gust of his breath seeps out of his turban and tickles your nose. You blink slowly, stepping backward.

The soldier grips your hair and jerks you toward him while your limbs remain frozen at your sides. You can barely feel the pain. It's just like a prick, nothing more.

"Listen here, *boy*," he spits, "I don't care who you think you are, breaking laws and being such a hero. You're living in ISIS territory and when you live in ISIS territory, you follow ISIS rules."

The soldier pulls on your hair harder until your eyes are an inch away from his. "You're going to go home *right now*, pack up and come to me, or else–"

He pauses, sliding a finger along your neck. "You should know what happens when you disobey authority."

The man lets go of your hair and rubs his hand against his suit. A patch of black flutters to the ground next to him. The second you turn, a harsh grip spins you around. An iron fist smacks your face and you stumble backward. The world begins to spin but you force yourself to turn back just as you were a couple of seconds before.

"This is just a fraction, *a fraction*, of what you'll get if you're not back here soon. I don't care what excuses you'll have. I'll cut your tongue out of that mute mouth of yours and then you'll be what you're pretending to be," the soldier calls out as his voice grows distant with each step you take.

laila

"LOOK, BABA." AMIR holds out his new clothes. Baba runs his fingers through the cloth.

"They look amazing. And the colors suit you too."

Amir rolls his eyes. "That's what you say every time, Baba."

"I don't," Baba sputters. Everyone's plates are empty now, a couple of sips left in Baba and Amir's cups. I stare at my glass, which lies untouched.

"Why do you save up your water? It's not like it's going anywhere. What difference does it make to drink it throughout the meal or all at once after?" Amir asks.

I shrug my shoulders. There's so little of everything here, barely enough to survive. Mixing the taste of the bread and the water together means a mash of flavors. I want to savor one thing at a time. Appreciate everything for what it is. Remember the joy of the first sip of water when I die.

"Laila. *Laila.*"

"Hm?"

Baba's warm, brown eyes meet mine. "Finish drinking and go to bed. You look like you haven't slept in years."

I nod. I clutch the glass in my hands and take the first sip. The lukewarm liquid swirls in my mouth, healing the raw skin inside my throat. I slurp a little more.

"Drink faster," Amir whines.

Baba puts a hand on Amir's shoulder. "Let her be. You go wash your face in that time."

Amir grimaces but walks toward the bathroom and closes the door behind him. Baba rests his head on his hand and stares at me.

"What?" I ask, water gurgling from under my tongue.

Baba's eyes don't budge. My stomach begins to twist. "Nothing. Just trying to make you uncomfortable."

"It's not working.".

"Are you sure about that? I think it is."

I shake my head and he sighs. "If you say so."

I slowly take my last sip, holding it in my mouth. The water grows warm inside and my cheeks begin to burn but I cherish the rare liquid. Baba's eyes are still locked on me and he chuckles. I shrug my shoulders.

Click.

The bathroom door swings open. Amir's face glimmers slightly in the candle light, a couple of drops streaming down his neck. He sticks his head forward. "You're still drinking?" he gawks.

Baba's mouth cracks open, laughing. "You should know by now that she is something else."

"But not like this," Amir exclaims. I narrow my eyes at him. "Don't look at me like that."

Baba bends down and stacks our plates on top of each other. "Alright now. Amir, in bed. Laila, wash up."

I latch onto the pile. "I got it."

Baba shakes his head. "I'm doing it. It's good for me anyway. Makes my muscles useful."

He steps up and his face contorts in pain, his hand jumping to his back. He flashes a smile at me. A pang of regret pricks my heart. If only I told him to take care of his health. If only I forced him to eat and drink more. If only I let him rest rather than crying about my small problems.

If.

If.

If.

"Now, hurry up or else, I'll take my sweet time in the bathroom."

"Baba," Amir cries from his bed. "Give me a hug."

Baba places the plates on the counter and swats the crumbs off with his hands. "I'm coming."

"If you don't hurry and I fall asleep without a hug, I'll have nightmares."

"We can't have that, can we?" Baba jogs over to Amir's bed and bends down to peck his hair. I catch him grunting as he stands back up. "Good night."

"Good night," Amir chirps before closing his eyes. Baba skips toward the kitchen and wraps his arms around me, my face digging into his ribs. He rubs my shoulders.

"My wonderful daughter," he whispers into my ear.

I pat his back, inhaling his sweet, musky scent. "I love you."

"I love you more."

He breaks away and his eyes flicker toward the bathroom. A sly smile buds on his face.

"Don't-"

Baba darts toward the door. "Too late," he sings, the wood of the door closing in my face. He swings it back right before it slams into my nose.

"Just kidding."

samira

THE DOOR WEEPS open. Yusuf throws his torn shoes off and places the loaves on the counter. A layer of thick dirt cakes the sides of the bread.

I cock my head and turn toward Yusuf, catching his face. From behind his curtain of hair, red peeks out. I brush it aside, a gasp erupting from my throat. The left side of his face is swollen and red, one of his eyes almost completely shut.

He walks straight past me. I reach for his wrist. "What. Happened?"

He remains frozen in place.

"Who did this?" I demand, my voice rising with each word.

Yusuf shrugs.

"What do you mean 'I don't know?' How do you not know who did this? Why did you let them?"

I brush my fingers against the stiff bump. Yusuf doesn't grimace, doesn't flinch, doesn't do anything. I gape at him. "Ice. We need ice. Why didn't I think of this before?"

I let go of Yusuf and throw open the fridge doors only to be welcomed by the darkness inside. It's just as hot as the rest of the house. I pat my face.

"Okay, okay. Water. Put water on it." I shake Yusuf's arm, my nails digging into his bones. "Water. Go to the bathroom and wash it."

Yusuf still doesn't budge. I push him into the bathroom and crack the faucet open, running my hand in the water until it's lukewarm. But it's only at room temperature for a couple of seconds before it's boiling all over again.

I scoop some of the liquid and press my hand against Yusuf's cheek. The water drips down his face. I do it again and again but it doesn't help. I turn the knob and the stream trickles until it's nothing.

"Yusuf, what happened?" He shrugs his shoulders but his eyes are lost, staring into space. I shake his shoulders.

"What. Happened?"

His eyes continue rattling and his mouth is slightly ajar. I touch the bump again but it's just as hard as it was before.

"*Yusuf,*" I cry. His eyes dart toward me. "Who did this? What did they do?"

He opens his mouth just a little. "ISIS."

My brain electrocutes.. "Why would they do that?"

He's dazed again.

"*Yusuf, why would they do that?*"

Pain shoots through my left arm and I grip my shoulder.

He glances from my hand to my face. "I'm eighteen," he says blankly.

"Did you tell them that?" The pain in my shoulder is now searing-white. The bathroom begins to blur. Yusuf's black hair expands and contracts, turning into monstrous curls. The white sink bounces up and down. The walls begin to close in. My heartbeat *thumps* in my ears.

Yusuf nods slightly.

yusuf

AUNT SAMIRA'S EYES flicker to the ceiling and her throat bubbles with raspy, gurgling sounds. Her knees collapse and she clenches her chest before she slumps onto the floor.

You strain to move your arms but they refuse, hanging limply by your sides. You try to move your tongue but it's useless inside your mouth.

It's your fault.

It's your fault.

It's your fault.

Aunt reaches into her pocket and stuffs an inhaler into her mouth. She breathes in deeply and releases her grip on her arm, letting it fall to the side.

You should have been more careful. You should have been quiet. You should never have come back. You should, you should, you should.

Because it's all your fault.

A couple of minutes later, she opens her eyes and curls into herself, head now resting against the cabinet under the sink.

"Are you okay?" you croak.

She smiles at you, a tender smile. She bobs her head slightly and then closes her eyes again.

Her voice is strained, as if there's a shard of glass piercing her throat. "Why did you tell them?"

The back of your eyes tingle and you clench your jaw. But you can't control the water from dripping out. Aunt pulls you down and wraps her arms around you. You hang your head on her shoulder, arms rocking back and forth. She pats your back gently.

"It's okay. They don't know where you live. We'll be safe."

"I'm sorry," you whisper. You pull from her embrace.

She shakes her head. "Don't be sorry. It's not your fault I have heart disease."

But it is. It's your fault she almost had a heart attack. It's your fault she had to worry. It's your fault she's stuck living like this.

This whole thing is your fault.

"Come with us to the bazaar," Mahmoud asks, his tiny hands clasped to your knee.

"Go with them, Yusuf. It'll be good for you," Mama says, her hand resting on your shoulder. Your dad nods and smiles, his mustache crinkling.

"I'm—I'm fine, really," you mutter.

"Are you sure?" Mama asks.

You nod, keeping your eyes trained on the floor. Mahmoud squeezes your leg harder. His glossy eyes peer up at you. "Please come. Maybe we'll see a dinosaur."

Baba smiles at me. "I know it's not much," he says, "To go buy bread but we have to try to make as much of it as we can. After all, no one is promised tomorrow. Let's go." Baba tosses you your shoes.

They land on the floor with a thud. That thud cracks something inside you. It boils deep inside your stomach, a fire sparking to life. You want to stay home, to stay away from the heat but no matter where you go, you can never escape your situation.

Something hard taps against your knee. You glance down to find Mahmoud's dinosaur attacking your knees.

"Raar. I'm a stegosaurus and I'm going to eat you," he growls.

The fire explodes.

"Dinosaurs don't exist, Mahmoud. How many times do I have to tell you? They died before any of us were alive."

Baba's eyebrows furrow together and his eyes are hard. Mama slips her shoes on and leads Mahmoud away from you. "Come on. How about I go with you guys?" Baba's eyes widen but she rests a hand on his arm. "I won't leave the car. Besides, they should be okay with it since I'll be with you."

Splat.

You can hear the echo of Mahmoud's tears hitting the tile floor. Baba lifts him up and places him on his shoulder. "Maybe we'll find another dinosaur," he says.

"Really?" Mahmoud mutters, sniffling. He looks at Mama. She nods enthusiastically.

Your mouth can't help but open. "We're in the middle of a civil war. You'll be lucky if you find food, let alone a toy dinosaur."

You jerk backward once the words flow out of your mouth. Mama snaps her head toward you, her pupils on fire and her teeth sinking into her lips.

"We're all living in this war. Every single one of us. Is it wrong to be hopeful? Is it?" Mama bursts.

Before you can even blink, the front door thunders shut.

laila

Baba's pocket begins to vibrate. He slides his hand inside and walks toward the bathroom door. "Give me a minute. Hello?"

He closes the door behind him as soon as the voice on the other side bursts to life. His muffled voice bounces off the thick walls. A couple of minutes later, he emerges, reaching toward the side of his bed for his briefcase. "I need to go to work. They need me early."

Amir whimpers beside me. Baba's eyes soften. "But that means I can come back home early tomorrow and with more money." He raises his eyebrows. "I'll buy some meat on the way and we can feast."

"What kind of meat?" Amir squeaks.

"Whatever you want."

Amir perks up. "Goat."

"Laila, what do you think?" I nod and he slips his feet into his shoes. "Go to sleep for a few more hours. I'll be back before you know it in sha Allah."

"Bye," Amir and I call out. Baba smiles warmly at us, his eyes closing as he does. The door *clicks* in place.

.   .   .

"Do you want to go outside with me?" Amir asks.

I shake my head. "I feel like staying in the shade today."

"But it's just as hot in here as it is outside," he whines.

"At least the sun isn't cooking me inside."

He pouts. "Fine. I'm going then."

I slide onto my bed. The sunlight blinks through the crack above the curtains, where the rod still sags. I drag a chair toward it and push the nail inside its socket, the rod straightening itself out. The sliver of light disappears.

I rest my hand against the sandy wall, and reach underneath my mattress, fingers trailing a strangled tube.

"The water is so pretty," I gasp. The sun's white light glimmers off the greenish-blue surface, sparkling like a jewel. A couple of gray birds dance in the sky, weaving between the clouds. My feet sink into the toasted sand.

Mama appears next to me, Amir strapped to her chest. Baba holds a blanket and a drooping bag. I touch the cloth. "What's in here?"

Baba smiles. "A surprise."

Mama rolls her eyes. "It's not that big of a surprise."

Baba pouts. "I want her to find out later, when we eat."

I clutch Baba's arm and jump up and down. "What is it? What is it?"

He chuckles. "You'll see. Now go on and play in the water before we have to go back home."

"Wait," Mama orders, "Don't forget your sunscreen."

I spin backward, eyes catching on the baby blue tube in her fingers. I stomp my foot. "I don't want it. It feels weird."

Mama shakes her head and squeezes a dollop of the white liquid into her palm. "You don't want to get cancer when you get older. Then, you'll wish that you had listened to your mother when you were younger."

I step toward her, sticking my face out. Mama's silky hands rub my skin violently. I squirm. "Stop moving. I'm almost done."

"What's cancer?" My words come out jumbled as Mama rubs my cheeks.

"A disease. A lot of people die because of it every day," she says.

"Will I get it?"

"God forbid. That's why you have to take care of yourself." Her hands move toward Amir's face. "Some for you too."

He thrashes against her chest, head jerking from side to side as she paints his face white. "Almost done. Almost done."

He sticks his lower lip out, his eyes glistening like the sea beside us. He buries his face in Mama's chest, his breath hitching. She rubs his back. "It's okay. Mama's done now."

I point at him. "See, even he doesn't like it."

Mama smiles. "One day, you both will realize but right now, it doesn't matter. You have to listen to me anyway."

I cross my arms over my chest. "When I'm a grown up, I'll do whatever I want and my first rule will be not to wear sunscreen."

Mama laughs. "Even when you're older, you'll still have to listen to me because I'll still be your mom."

"We'll see about that."

Mama's hand nudges me forward. "Now, go into the water. It'll feel good in this heat."

samira

I GAZE OUT the window. The sky is pitch black, a couple of stars peeking from behind a veil of clouds. A gentle glint of moonlight catches the side of my eye and I turn, examining the two frames on my bedside table.

The wood frame of one is splintered from the corner, the glass encasing the picture a little cloudy. Inside is Mama, Baba, my brother and me. Baba scratches his beard, his eyes widened as he sees the shutter of the camera blink. Mama is smiling but her hands are tucking the tufts of loose hair behind my ear. My brother is grinning, his eyes closed as the corners of his mouth reach them.

I'm pouting. My arms are crossed and my lower lip juts out, all because Mama had refused to buy me a doll, saying I had too many. I vowed to ruin her picture then.

I chuckle at the memory. How Mama hung the picture on her wall, despite my horrific facial expression. How she stared at it as the cancer forced her to draw her last breath. How Baba died in the middle of the night, his arms wrapped around that picture. How my brother might have relived that very memory during his last heartbeat.

I turn to the other frame. Zayd and I stand, one arm looped around the other's back. Zayd is in a gray thawb with gold thread sewn on the collar. I'm in a light green dress, a hint of brown embroidery at the cuffs of my sleeves. Our heads rest against each other and our smiles reach our eyes.

I reach out and brush my finger against the glass, against Zayd's face.

Zayd crouches so I don't have to look up with my heavy eyes. He clears his throat. "This is my promise on our wedding day. I won't let this war ruin anything. It doesn't matter who invades the city and when another bombing will occur. I will make sure you and our children are sheltered from it forever."

My vision is blurred now and a gentle stream flows down my face. I take a deep breath, steadying my thoughts. I will keep Yusuf safe, even if he doesn't want me to.

.   .   .

I dig the knife into a loaf of bread, watching as the blade slides out clean. The slice flops to the side and waits for its companion to join. I spread a smudge of hummus on top.

"Yusuf, time to eat," I call.

I crack open the door before he responds. Yusuf is in bed, his eyes locked together and his mouth shut tightly. His hands and neck are hugging his blanket, his fingers white from holding on.

I crouch and place the plate near his head. I push his shoulders. "Wake up. Time for dinner."

He shifts toward the wall, covering his eyes with his arm. "It'll just take a minute and then you can go to sleep."

He shakes his head. I pull his arm off his face. "I'm not leaving until you eat."

"Not hungry," he whispers.

"You are hungry," I say. I slip my fingers underneath his back and pull him up. His eyes are red and the skin underneath them is purple and swollen.

"Eat," I command. He hesitates, before nibbling on the slice.

I nod and ruffle his hair. He pushes my hand away, gluing his body to the wall so he's as far away from me as possible.

Thud.

My ears perk up. I saunter to the front door. Outside, someone climbs the stairs of the apartment building, their footsteps growing louder and louder.

My heart matches the steps.

Thud.

THUD.

And then, they stop.

The silence rings in my ears. I get on my knees and peer through the crack under the door. Two black boots stare back. A second later, they turn to face the neighbor's house.

Then they flip back. My breath catches in my throat, making a *hich* sound. I snap my head toward Yusuf's room. Slow raps on the door echo throughout the house.

Knock. Knock.

A minute of silence.

Knock. Knock.

The knocks are louder this time. "Open the door," a voice calls out.

Knock. Knock.

"I hear you in there."

yusuf

YOU SWING AWAY from the wall, the light from the door stinging your eyes. You crack them open a bit. Aunt is on her knees with her head cocked toward your room. Her eyes are wide and wild while her mouth hangs open. A thunderous knocking echoes throughout the house.

You tiptoe toward the door. Aunt shakes her head and puts a finger on her lips.

KNOCK. KNOCK.

Your fingers remain wrapped around the bumpy wall. Aunt swings her hands violently but your eyes are glued to the trembling door. The doorknob rattles, its nails clinking against the metal.

"I'm going to break this door down," the voice from outside growls.

Aunt tumbles off the floor and into the hallway, wrenching the door away from you and slamming it closed. You lean your head against the wall, closing your eyes. The front door creaks open.

"What took you so long?" A male voice booms.

"Sorry, sorry, I was using the bathroom," Aunt says.

The man shuffles and there's a long pause. "I've got reports of a young man living here."

"A young man?...Oh, that must be my nephew. He was visiting but he went back to Damascus with his parents a couple days ago. Why would you want him?"

Shoes scuff the tile floor, the screeching taking over your ears. A door creaks open.

"Excuse me?" Aunt's voice is just a gentle ring in the air. "Isn't it improper for you to go into my room? I'd like my privacy to be respected."

The man scoffs. "Privacy? There's no such thing as *privacy* here. It doesn't matter what *private* things are in there. Try to stop me and I'll arrest you within a second. Understand?"

Crash. THUD. THUD.

The walls crack and tremble as objects fling into them. The movements travel down your head and neck. Your fingers and teeth clatter.

The earthquake pauses, giving way to voices. "What's in that room?" the man demands.

"The guest room," Aunt mutters.

"What's in the *guest room?*"

"Just a mattress. My nephew was staying there while his parents conducted business."

"And what business would that be?"

"Hm?" Aunt says.

"What business would that be?"

"I don't know."

Screee.

A deafening, piercing sound rips my ears. "How would you not know?"

Aunt's words slur into one another, her tongue rattling as fast as it can. "Th-They didn't tell me. It was some sort of business dealing. They were out most of the day and came back only to eat. They live in Damascus. I've never visited but you can look for them there if you want to ask them."

"You must know *something* about them." The soldier's voice is now thin and sly.

"No, I really don't. If I knew anything, I'd tell you. I wanted to know what they were doing too but they refused to tell me."

"You should know that you should report illegal activity," the soldier snaps.

"I-It never crossed my mind. Really, it didn't. They're housing contractors. I thought they were scoping the area to build houses."

"They stayed in the guest room?"

Aunt doesn't say anything. The door pops open and she steps inside. Her eyes flicker toward you but she spins around, pressing the door into your curled-up body and stepping in front of the gap.

"Here's the guest room."

Through a sliver of space to Aunt's right, a tall, sturdy man steps through the door. His eyes are a piercing gray, bringing out the hint of white in his hair. Lines run along his cheeks, crinkling every time he breathes. His hands rest on his belt that holds two knives and a pistol.

Your brain lights up. If he sees you, he'll shoot you right away. And then this will all be over. You shift a bit but Aunt twists to cover you.

He turns toward your bed. "Why isn't this made?"

Aunt's fingers twist behind her back. "I didn't have time to make it. I've been busy redecorating the house and spending time with my husband, Zayd."

The soldier crosses his arms. Aunt leans back, the air around you growing thick.

The man's voice drops, the entire apartment quivering with it. "Where is your money?"

Aunt freezes. "What?"

The man glares at her with hard, narrowed eyes. "Where is your *money?*"

"Wh-"

"*Where. Is. Your. Money?*" Drops of spit spray from his mouth.

"I don't know."

"You're lying."

"No, I really don't have money," Aunt pleads. "I really don't. We can barely afford to eat once a day. How could we have money?"

The soldier lurches for her arm and puts his face inches from hers. "Surely, your *husband* must have some emergency funds somewhere. I'll have both of you killed on the spot and that money will be mine anyway so I'll ask nicely one more time. Where is the money?"

Aunt's voice is hoarse. "My-my closet. In the back."

The soldier's eyes light up and he spins on his heels. Heavy footsteps echo throughout the room. A door slams open.

Aunt appears in the doorway and grips your wrist. "Go, go, go," she whispers. You freeze and her mouth pulls into a line. "Go."

She huffs, right before pushing you out of the apartment and down the stairs. The stiff air outside clogs your lungs while the sun cackles. You glance at Aunt's hand wrapped around your numb wrist.

She ducks into an alley beside the apartment building and shoves you behind a pile of bricks.

"Don't say a word," she whispers and burrows right next to you. You blink and the darkness closes in, wrapping its icy hands around your neck. It stuffs itself into your veins, your heart resisting. The air begins to boil.

Aunt rubs your arm. "It's okay. It's okay."

The world starts to spin, warping into beasts of different shapes and sizes. Tears cloud your vision and your chest tightens.

Aunt wraps her arms around you. "It's okay. It's okay." The black starts to retreat a bit, cowering from Aunt's light. But it lingers in the corners, waiting to pounce. Aunt picks strands of stray, wet hair from your face.

Footsteps thunder down the street.

"Hey, *hey*. There's a lady who's on the loose somewhere here. She ran from her house while I was searching. I repeat, we have a lady, a possible spy, on the loose." The soldier's voice drowns in the wind.

Aunt bristles besides you. "Go to sleep," she whispers. "We'll leave after sunset."

She nudges your head against a barrel and pats your arm slowly, just like your mother used to when you were little.

laila

THE SKY OUTSIDE wears its darkest shade, not a single star glimmering in sight. I pull my legs to my chest, feet resting on the boiling tile floor beneath the foam mattress. Beside me, Amir's mouth hangs open to the side and his breath scratches against his lungs. One of his fingers is curled around my blanket, stroking it as if it were a lost cat.

I rest my chin on my knees. My eyes sink into their sockets and my knuckles are bleached from gripping my elbows. The mat in front of the door lies empty. The only sign of life outside is the breeze rattling against the windows.

Amir stirs beside me, rolling onto my mattress. I rest my arm over his back, patting it slowly, just like Mama used to. The muscles on his face loosen a bit. The numbers on the clock glare at me.

1:18 A.M.

My head perks up, Baba's distant voice ringing in my ears.

"I have to go to work now, okay?" Baba says, holding his briefcase close to himself.

"Can I come with you?"

He smiles. "No, Laila. You can't."

I tug on his sleeve, fingers brushing against the cool buttons on his cuff. I peer up, his beard an expanding bush on his face. "Please?"

He turns toward the counter, places his bag on it and lifts me up. My legs wrap around his waist and I grip onto his neck. "Laila, if I don't go to work, we won't have money to buy bread. The office is no place for children to be. You've always wanted to be a big girl, right? I need you to act like a big girl so you can take care of your brother."

I lace my fingers into his hair. "But I don't want you to leave me."

He smiles sadly. "I know. I don't want to go but I have to."

I shake my head. "No, you don't."

"Then where will we get money from?"

I tilt my head to the side, my lips glued together. "I don't know."

"See?"

I look down. "When will you come back?"

"Before you go to sleep," he says.

"Do you promise?" I whisper.

Baba holds his pinky out in the little space between us. "I promise I'll always be there to tuck you into bed."

Yet, this is the first time he hasn't come back since that promise. Tears prick my eyes. Amir scootches closer to me, his legs now bumping mine. He curls his arms toward himself and rubs his face against my shirt, licking his cracked lips.

"Look, Laila. There's the beach. There's water." He pauses. "Look, Baba. There's Mama. Mama. Mama."

My stomach knots itself. Mama's not here. She's gone. My head hangs to the side, my limbs growing heavy and numb. The dim halo of the moon lights the room through the sheet above me, landing on the glass frame near my hand.

I pick it up, the figures blurring in and out of focus. Mama, Amir and I splash each other with the bejeweled salt water. A couple of drops stain the camera lens, distorting the red sun behind us. Mama's grin glows in the light while Amir's face is like a tomato, his mouth wide open to holler. I'm leaning backward, my arms outstretched in front of me. In the corner, there's a brief flash of reddish-white, a tiny figment of Baba.

samira

YUSUF'S HEAD leans back against a brick wall. His mouth is cracked open and soft snores resonate from his mouth.

I glance up at the sky. It's getting dark, the perfect time for us to slip out of Raqqa. I tap his arm. "Yusuf, wake up. We have to go now."

He shifts a little. "Come on. Wake up," I plead.

His eyes jerk open but he doesn't move.

"Yusuf, I don't think you understand the situation we're in. We're *wanted.* All the soldiers in

Raqqa are looking for us. We need to get out of the city if we want to live."

He shakes his head ever so slightly.

"You don't have a choice in this matter. We're leaving and that's that."

He narrows his eyes. A muscle in his neck vibrates. I pull myself off the ground, waiting for my tight muscles to relax. Yusuf just glares at me.

I grip his arm. "We're leaving now."

But no matter how hard I pull, he's glued to the ground.

"Yusuf, please, don't make this hard. You know we have to leave. That soldier is out for our blood. If he finds out that you're living with me and not enlisted, he'll kill both of us."

Yusuf shakes his head and crosses his arms across his chest. His fingers grip his biceps, his shirt crinkling together as he does.

"Please."

He shakes his head again and stares at the wall in front of us. I wave my hand in front of his eyes but they remain fixed in their place.

"Yusuf, *Yusuf.*"

He doesn't look at me. I groan. "What would your parents want?"

His eyes snap toward me. "Your parents would want you to live. Maybe you don't but it's my job now to protect you. I won't let you die. I won't."

I gaze into his eyes. They're empty and heavy now, a slight shine coming from them. I tug on his arm and this time, he doesn't resist.

I nudge him forward. "Let's go."

.   .   .

Past the city, a sea of sand lies beyond the stream ahead of us. A couple of barren, dead trees spring out in the middle of the yellow but they're just silhouettes in the darkness. The blanket of stars above cast light on the two armed figures stationed to the left and right.

I glance over my shoulder, at houses on the horizon. If I strain hard enough, I can hear Couscous ruffling his feathers. I can hear him purring as he waits for me to sprinkle seeds in his cage. My chest tightens and I stroke my hand, almost feeling Couscous' feathers.

I press my nail into my thumb. If we walk past Raqqa's borders, the soldiers will see us and shoot.

"We need to crawl," I whisper to Yusuf. He turns toward me slightly but his eyes are still as empty as they were before. I push his shoulder down and he folds to the ground, landing on his hands and knees. I tap the torn sole of his shoe and he inches forward. The grass rustles under our bodies.

Krrr. Krr.

"Who's there?" a gruff voice calls out. The air in my lungs freezes. I push myself on top of Yusuf, pressing him into the ground.

Bang. Bang.

I flinch, the grass rustling even more. I cup my ears.

Bang. Bang.

"I will keep firing and I *will* catch you."

Bang.

A bullet flies right past my ear. I roll off Yusuf and push against his shoes. He starts to crawl.

"I hear you."

Bang. Bang. Bang.

I dig my fingers into the dirt and pull myself up.

Bang. Bang. Bang. Bang.

I clap my hands over my ringing ears.

Faster.

Faster.

Faster.

My muscles burn, threatening to rip off my bones. Just one more push.

I let myself loose, my arms throbbing and my tongue dry. The gunshots are faint noises in the breeze now. I tear myself off the floor. Yusuf is still on the ground, his head resting against the dirt. I hold my hand out to him.

"Let's go," I whisper.

Yusuf stands up with the dirt still clinging to his shirt, not even glancing at my extended hand.

yusuf

LIGHT TICKLES YOUR skin. You shift a bit, watching as the world zooms beside you. You squeeze your eyes but when you open them, the houses are still flying.

You lean forward and something catches you in the chest. You glance down at the gray strip digging into your stomach and neck. You grip it, pulling but it refuses to move. You squirm but the seatbelt bites deeper and deeper.

You snap your head to the side. Brown and gray blurs sprint past you, cackling as they do. The road beneath you is just a haze.

Panic begins to flood into your throat. Gentle laughter echoes beside you. You jerk your head to the side to find Mahmoud's toy dinosaur tapping the window. A delicate hand brings the toy back and forth, and Mahmoud's laughter grows louder with each moment.

Your breath hitches. You peer toward the front of the vehicle to find Mama smiling at Mahmoud, her eyes tender and warm. Baba's eyes are fixed on the road but his grin reflects off the rearview mirror.

"*No, no, no,*" you scream. Your fingers tug on the seat belt but it refuses, hugging you tighter and tighter until you can't breathe.

Boom.

The car is thrown across the street like a ragdoll. The whole world spins.

And then, time slows down. Each muscle is visible to you, every movement pronounced. Mahmoud screams, his dinosaur flung toward the back. Tears run down his cheeks while his mouth is wide open. Mama lurches to grab him but her fingers barely brush his shirt. Baba's hands fly to the dashboard, moving in a frenzy across the buttons of the car. You slip your hands in front of Mahmoud but he slides right through them.

"*No,*" you cry. But Mahmoud slams into the front seat.

Crash.

Everything speeds up. The car slams into the ground, the floor crumpling beneath you. And then you're rolling again and again and again until...

Everything stops.

The entire vehicle is filled with thick, black smoke that infects your lungs. You grip your throbbing head and blink. Your feet are above your head, your arms brushing against the car's roof that's now underneath you.

You blindly jab at the seat belt button but it's dead. The clip is lodged so deep it's barely visible. You reach around and your hands rub against something warm and wet. You bring your arm back toward your face.

And it's red.

You shriek, smoke stinging your eyes. It's pitch black and the outline of silhouettes grows crips. Mahmoud is dangling in the air, kept afloat by what remains of his seatbelt. His legs are twisted together. Mama is stretched between the front and the back of the car. Her arm is just an inch away from Mahmoud and her neck is turned so sharply, it looks like it snapped off her head. Baba's head is smushed against the steering wheel, a cloud of red is painted across the black wheel.

Vomit floods into your mouth and it sprays out. A whiff of smoke, laced with the smell of blood, fire and vomit sears your nose. You recoil your legs and slam them against the door but it refuses to budge. You kick again and again but it just screams in pain. The air around you grows hot and thick. You run the back of your hand against your chin and punch the window.

"Open, open, *open.*"

But the glass remains as it is. Fire surges through your veins. You thrash, kick, punch and slam against the door but it doesn't give in.

And then you stop.

You let your head loose and sob.

And sob.

And sob.

Your heart contracts with pain, begging you to stop but you can't.

You just can't.

Creak.

You jerk your head upward. The wall to your left inches toward you. You turn to the other side. Mahmoud, Mama and Baba have vanished, streaks of blood being the only sign of their existence.

Crack.

All of a sudden, the car squeezes itself into a ball, compressing tighter. You kick the window and scream, begging for it to open. The boiling metal caresses your arm and you flinch. Your leg goes numb. You glance up toward it to find it engulfed in the hot metal.

You strain, the walls creeping closer and closer. The car begins to chew your leg. A whimper escapes your lips. You wrap your arms around your head. Beads of sweat drip down your face.

Your arms are forced into your stomach, only a few millimeters between you and the metal. Something bites into your hand. You peer down to find fire licking at your fingers.

A scream erupts from your throat.

laila

AMIR'S EYES FLUTTER open, his hazy pupils darting back and forth. "What time is it?"

"2:47."

"In the morning? Then where's Baba?"

I shake my head. Amir props himself up, his eyes terrified. "Where is he?"

"I don't know," I whisper.

He shrinks a little, his head sinking into his neck. "It's late. He said he would be back home early. Do you know where he works?"

"No...We stopped asking after all those transfers."

"So we have no idea where he is," Amir whispers.

"Let's go look for him," I say. Amir looks up and he nods. He pushes himself off the mattress, pulling his arms high above his head, and rubs his eyes.

I jump off my bed and sprint toward the door until my fingers curl around the knob, the steamy metal searing my skin. The air outside is tense, as if waiting for an attack while the city is quiet. I scan the houses around me, eyeing their drawn curtains and shut doors.

Amir steps beside me, the door closing behind him. "Let's go," he murmurs, fatigue laced in his voice.

We begin to weave through the streets, my eyes scanning the homes and buildings throughout the city but not a single light is lit. The offices' half torn towers are silent, except for the gentle scurry of mice and insects. Otherwise, the town is asleep.

Amir nods toward me. "You look there and I'll look over there," he says right before running off.

Over the next three hours, we check everywhere: behind barrels, inside buildings, under rocks. But Baba's nowhere. Soon, the sun begins to ascend from its slumber, the sky erupting into shades of orange and red. Amir and I perch on a half-broken wall. "We've searched everywhere," I mutter.

Amir stiffens. "At least three times. Was Baba working out of town?"

I shrug my shoulders, a needle pricking the back of my eyes. Amir clears his throat. "Maybe he's at home and we don't know because we're here. Maybe he forgot to come back early. Or maybe he's working late and can't tell us."

"Maybe," I whisper. But deep down, I know that's not the case.

We trudge down the street. Amir's feet drag across the dust, sending it dancing in the air. As soon as he sees our house, he sprints forward toward and throws the door open. I peek inside but it's just as we left it. Empty.

I glance at the mat, where Baba's shoes are still missing.

"He might be in the bathroom," I mutter. I push open the bathroom, only to find no one. Absolutely no one.

Amir's eyes glimmer. "He could be staying somewhere tonight. He'd want to tell us but he couldn't because there's no phone."

"But what if he's not?"

Amir inhales sharply. "What do you mean?"

I push my voice out. "What if he's not staying somewhere?"

"Then where would he be?"

"I don't know," I cry, my eyes fixed on the floor. Amir's mouth zips tight. "I don't know."

"You don't think he left us, do you?" he whispers.

I look up at Amir's glimmering eyes. My throat is sandy, his words bouncing inside my head.

Left.

Left.

Left.

"Baba would never leave us. *Never*," I whisper.

Amir's voice is a little stronger now. "How do you know?"

"Because he promised," I burst.

"When kids are young, their parents promise them everything, including the impossible. Baba has been saving money for airplane tickets. Don't you think he would have had enough for at least one person? Wouldn't you want to leave this place too?"

I shake my head and glare at Amir's stone eyes. "He would never leave us behind. He would never abandon us."

"But what if he would?"

My chest is pounding, ringing in my ears. "You're just saying things."

Amir shakes his head.

"Then give me proof," I growl.

"I heard him." He pauses for a second, weaving his fingers into one another. "I heard him talking on the phone one night. About visas and plane tickets and prices. The man said something on the phone and Baba said yes, that he wanted to leave."

All the air in my lungs evaporates and my heart buries itself into my stomach, vowing to never come back up. The prick at the back of my eyes is now spreading, clouding my eyes. Amir's body distorts into a blob.

Arms wrap around my shoulders and my face rubs against Amir's chest. He strokes my head. "Shhh."

"Did he really leave us?" I sob.

Amir is quiet. My breath hitches in my throat. "He really left, right? He really abandoned us."

"It's okay. It's okay."

I struggle in Amir's grip but he squeezes tighter. My words come out jumbled. "He promised. He promised to always come back. He promised he'd never leave. He promised."

I cup my hands over my face, fingers soaking the tears. "He had a choice and he chose," Amir gulps.

I hiccup. "We weren't part of that choice." I pause. "But why would he do that? Why?"

"I don't know," he says.

"Tell me why."

"If I knew, I would tell you. You know I would tell you. I tell you everything."

"I want him back. I want Baba back."

Amir continues rubbing my back while my tears drip through the cracks in my fingers and down my arms.

samira

YUSUF JERKS STRAIGHT up, a scream ripping from his throat. A thick sheen of sweat glistens on his skin. His chest rises and falls rapidly while his eyes race from side to side.

I jolt, my arms shielding my face. After a second, when my vision clears, I lean toward him and rub his back. "Shh. Shh. It's okay. It was just a dream," I say.

"Just a dream. Just a dream. Just a dream," he whispers.

"Yes, yes. Nothing more than a dream. Dreams aren't real."

"But they can be," he murmurs. He turns away from me, my fingers now rubbing the air. He rests his head on his knees and his eyes lose themselves in the expanse of sand.

My stomach purrs. My throat is dry, as if I swallowed a handful of dirt. I lean my head against a tree. Its thin, tiny leaves provide a slight refuge from the sun but the air is still thick with sweat.

The clouds above are stretched into lines. I watch as they chase each other. They're the only sign that the Earth is still alive. Everything else is so still, so dead.

I tilt my head to the left. If I squeeze my eyes hard enough, I can picture Raqqa: the gentle buzz of the suqq, the hum of cars, the blanket of peace.

The memories.

The memories I will never be able to return to. The home I've left behind. Couscous.

A sob climbs into my throat but I shake it away. I'm the adult here. I have to keep my emotions in check. If Yusuf and I both break down, there won't be anyone to think clearly.

My eyes grow heavy and I bite my tongue. Yusuf is still dazed, his hand brushing against the sand. "What are you thinking about?" I ask.

He shakes his head.

"You must be thinking about something."

He shakes his head again. I sigh. "You didn't want to leave. I know. I forced you to come with me and maybe you'll hate me for it. But we had to leave to survive."

I pause. "I know it's been hard for you. It's been difficult for me too, you know? He was my brother. The one person I had left. The one person who's been with me my entire life. He promised he was always going to stay. But you know there's a reason, a hidden blessing. We just have to seek it out. We have to find that little glint of hope."

Yusuf stares at the grains of sand on his fingers. "I don't know," he whispers.

"Just try. Try to find that glint, that hope. That's it."

He nods ever so slightly.

yusuf

AUNT SMILES AT you and you try to mimic it. But as soon as her eyes fall someplace else, your mouth drops.

Life is a gift. Life is *supposed* to feel like a gift. You have the chance to laugh, to cry, to love.

But now, it's a burden. A burden that makes your legs tremble and your joints crack. No matter how hard you try, it will never go away. While death used to tempt you before, it evades you now. It laughs at you, mocking your pathetic life.

And it's right. You lived when they died. You lived after you hurt them. You lived after you refused to cherish them.

You lived after you killed them.

Aunt shifts beside you, stretching her arms. "Let's go. We should try to find a city before it gets dark."

She holds out her hand but you refuse to take it.

. . .

Crunch. Crunch.

You whip backward at the gentle scurry of footsteps. Your eyes dart back and forth before they land on the figure near you. Your feet sink into the sand. Mahmoud trots behind you, his face glowing in the sun and his toy dinosaur in his hands. He waves at you eagerly.

Tears prick your eyes. Mahmoud's smile falters a little and he dashes toward you, his arms stretched wide. You catch him, squeezing his boney frame. You dig your face into his shoulder, gulping his scent of grapes and the ocean, fresh and salty. His tiny hands pat your shoulders and the tears break free.

"It's okay," Mahmoud whispers, his eyes shining as well. He wipes the tears with his sleeve.

"Can you come with me? Please?" Your hand grips him even tighter.

"Where are you going?"

"I don't know," you respond.

"Then why are you going?"

"Because—because it's dangerous to stay in Raqqa," you reply.

"Why?" he asks.

You smile. "I'll tell you tomorrow, once we're in a different city, okay?"

He nods and cocks his head, playing with his fingers. "What about Mama and Baba?"

Your voice cracks. "I don't know where they are."

Mahmoud rests his head on your shoulders. "They'll find us soon, right?"

You nod, your cheek on his. You close your eyes, sobs erupting from deep within your stomach.

"Don't cry," Mahmoud whines.

You chuckle. "Okay, okay. I'll try."

And then he's gone. Your arms are barren while your head rests against the breeze. You comb your eyes left and right, your heart trembling

THUMP. THUMP. THUMP.

Your knees are vibrating now, wobbling like a wave. The world around you begins to blur and your head grows heavy. Spots of black dance in front of you.

A hand rests on his arm. You spin toward it. "Mahmoud? Mahmoud?"

Your face drops when you meet Aunt's widened eyes. The tears drip uncontrollably, drenching your face, into your mouth and nose. You rub your fingers together, finding them just as wet.

"He was right here. He was right here," you croak.

Aunt Samira wipes your tears away with her fingers. "Where did he go?" you whisper.

She shakes her head. "I don't know. I don't know."

laila

I SLITHER OUT of Amir's grip, patting his back. He purrs a little and curls inward before his snores resume again. I tilt my head back, letting my skull rock back and forth against the wall. A drizzle of dust rains down from the opposite corner as the ceiling creaks just a little.

I reach for the frame beside my bed and hug it close to my chest. The skin under my eyes tingles but remains dry, not a single sign of a tear. I rub the tips of my fingers together, trying to burn the dryness off but it just laughs at me.

My heart winds itself in my veins. Baba couldn't have just left. He couldn't have. He would never abandon us. We're the only ones he's got left, the only reason for him to keep going.

He's the only reason I keep going.

But a voice in the back of my mind confirms what I already know. "He abandoned you," it hisses. "He doesn't love you. Why else would he be so desperate to run away? Why else would he have had that conversation Amir told you about? Stop deluding yourself."

I shrivel, flinching at the harsh words. My chest contracts. This is why hope is a mirage. It lures you in with its sweet voice, only to jam a knife through your back once you're deep in delusion. And when you see the blood pooling onto the ground, it's too late. By then, your soul is clawing its way out of your throat.

All you can do is regret. Regret ever playing hope's game in the first place. Promise yourself that you will never fall into that trap again.

samira

MY SKIN BURNS at the touch of the sun. The sand below me brands the soles of my feet. The sky, the ground, the air: all of it is yellow. Except for the line of black up ahead.

I shield my eyes and squint into the sunlight. A couple of figures stand erect in the middle of the desert. I turn to Yusuf. "Look. Look. There are people."

A grin spreads on my face. Yusuf glances toward them and nods, tilting his head back toward the ground. I grab his wrist and pull him behind me, my feet speeding up.

The figures grow crisper and crisper as we inch toward them. Each one is suited in green with turbans of brown or black wrapped around their faces. They turn to each other and one of them steps forward as soon as he sees us. Just like the rest of them, his eyes are the only thing visible. His sleeve is pulled up over his elbow, his veins bulging out of his arm.

"Where are you coming from?" he booms.

I glance toward Yusuf and back to the soldier, whose hands are now resting on the pistol on his belt.

"Where are you coming from?"

I blink.

"What?"

The soldier grimaces. "You both are coming from IS territory. Where exactly are you coming from?"

"Raqqa," Yusuf whispers beside me.

The soldier leans in. "Huh?"

"Raqqa," he whispers.

The soldier nods and rests his hands on his hips. "And why would you want to leave Raqqa? That must be your hometown, no?"

"It's dangerous. There are soldiers everywhere, watching our every move. There's not a second we're safe," I respond.

The soldier shifts his eyes toward me. "If you wanted to escape from ISIS, you would have left *years* ago. What's the real reason for your *escape?*"

"Officer, you have to understand. Raqqa is basically destroyed. No one is allowed to leave without being questioned. The soldiers there force people into joining the army. We were just trying to flee from all that."

The soldier's mouth tightens into a line. "Force, huh? Were you *forced?*"

I nod. "Yes. We were threatened if we didn't comply."

At the word "threatened," the soldier's head snaps toward me, his eyes narrowed. He steps forward.

"So you're telling me you had direct interaction with ISIS?"

I lean back, squeezing Yusuf's arm. "No, I—"

"Were you forced or not?"

"We were but—"

"Then why did you say no earlier?"

My chest contracts. "I-I-"

The man lowers his face until he's an inch away from mine. With each passing second, a gust of hot, sticky air from his nose blows into my face. I pull my head back, stifling a whimper.

He turns to his left. The yellow of the sand shines in his eyes. "You're still trying to lie to me," he mutters, calmly.

His head snaps toward me. His eyes are wild, darting from me to Yusuf. Yusuf keeps his face pointed toward the ground. His face is shielded by the locks of hair snaking down toward his feet.

The man straightens, towering over both of us. He jabs a finger at Yusuf. "You're a part of them, aren't you?"

Yusuf shakes his head. The soldier grips his shoulder and rattles him back and forth.

"Answer me."

Yusuf remains silent. The soldier takes a step forward, a smile spreading on his face. "You're not denying it." He tilts his head toward the sky and laughs.

I step backward, his voice ringing in my ears. The soldier inhales deeply.

"Don't try to escape." He meets my eyes. "There's only so long before we find you."

My legs freeze. The man reaches behind his back and the *clink* of metal echoes throughout the desert. "You're under arrest for committing terrorist activities."

"What?" I shriek. My heart begins to pound. "We're not terrorists. We haven't done anything wrong."

The man cocks his head to the side. "Prove it then."

I glance toward Yusuf, who's still staring at the ground with his mouth ajar. "We don't have anything on us. Not even a morsel of food. It's proof that we ran without looking back."

The soldier shakes his head. "That doesn't prove a thing."

He brings the handcuffs to my wrists. I pull them back. "We didn't do anything. We're not terrorists. We don't even know how to fight. We're just innocent people trying to find peace in—"

"Nobody is innocent," the man interrupts. The words in my mouth evaporate into the air, leaving behind only what could have been.

"Nobody is innocent in this world. Everyone has played a part, whether they know it or not. So you're not innocent. Those who are not innocent are guilty."

I step back, my ankle digging into my skirt. My chest contracts and a wave of pain surges. "No, no, no."

I look toward Yusuf, who still hasn't moved. I shake my head. The world begins to blur.

"No. No. *No.*"

The soldier grips my arms and I shriek. He pulls them behind me, the metal biting into my skin. I squirm but my wrists refuse to slide through the handcuffs. The man cocks an eyebrow at Yusuf.

Yusuf pulls his head up until it's level with the soldier's. With empty eyes, he glances toward his wrists and holds them up.

PART II

yusuf

THE SOLDIER PAUSES when he reaches the others.

"I caught some of the terrorists Commander Bilal warned us about. He was right. They'll pretend that they're fleeing from persecution when all they're waiting for is a chance to bomb our army and conquer all of Syria."

The other soldiers nod, smiles on their faces.

"Good job," someone booms from the back. Everyone spins and as soon as their eyes land on the figure, they raise their hands in salute.

A man limps toward the group. His fingers are curled around a cane while he leans to the right heavily. A black patch covers one of his eyes and a faint bush forms spikes on his chin.

He rests a hand on the man's shoulder. Aunt opens her mouth but he holds a finger in front of her.

"Now, now, no need to argue. I trust this man's judgment. If he said you're terrorists, then to me, you're terrorists."

The man beams. "Thank you, Commander."

"No—" Aunt begins but Commander Bilal jerks toward her.

"It seems you didn't understand me the first time. Let me say it again in *simpler* terms. No matter what you say, I won't let you go. You can scream, cry and argue as much as you want but you'll just be wasting your energy, not mine."

Bilal nods toward the man, whose eyes are shining. "Take them to the detention center."

Aunt's head snaps toward the commander. "Detention cen-No, no, no. Please. *Please,*" she cries.

You've heard of these detention camps built by the SDF. They're supposedly the "good guys," the rebels who started this whole war for democracy and peace. But you know better than to believe that. There are no good guys, not here in all places. You're not even good, let alone a good guy. You're a murderer and a murderer deserves to die.

Bilal turns back toward the direction he came from and walks off, not a single glance over his shoulder. The soldier pushes Aunt forward and she collapses onto her knees.

"Get up," the soldier barks.

"Please," she begs. Tears drip down her face.

"Get. Up."

The soldier pulls out his rifle and digs its mouth into Aunt's back. She freezes.

"Get up," he barks. Aunt rises off the ground and steps forward.

Up ahead, a black strip is paved between two sand mounds. It snakes through the desert, disappearing into the horizon. As you draw closer, the silhouette of a van grows crisp. A wisp of smoke gathers near the engine.

The man reaches over your shoulder and pulls on a handle. The vehicle's door slides open, the pitch black luring you in. You reach into the air and you watch your hand disappear, feeling your fingers curl but not seeing them.

You settle into the darkness.

At the entrance, Aunt freezes. The soldier *clicks* his gun and her face drains.

"You should get in," he whispers.

And then the door slams shut. The darkness swirls in front of you. Fingers brush against your hand.

"It's okay," Aunt's voice cracks. The black fades into gray and her outline grows crisp. She crawls toward the door and digs her fingers into the handle. She tilts to the other side, straining. After a couple of seconds, her fingers slip. Her handcuff chain *clinks* against the door.

She grunts and coils her legs.

Slam. Slam. Slam.

The whine of metal rings in your ears. Aunt kicks the door again and again but you know it won't work. It didn't work when you were trapped in that car in your dream. Nothing worked.

It's just like that.

THUD. THUD. THUD.

"Stop that."

Aunt crumples to the ground and weeps.

"I'm sorry I dragged you into this mess. We should have stayed." Her throat hitches. "I'm so sorry. I'm so sorry."

She curls into a ball and sobs into her knees. A lump lodges into your throat.

"I'm so sorry. I'm so sorry."

"It's okay," you croak.

"No, it's not. It's not. I just wanted to keep you safe." Her glistening eyes meet yours. "I wanted to give you a life. I wanted you to live like there is no war. Like we're all safe." She pauses. "I know it hurts. I know it hurts to move on. I know you don't want to live. I know it hurts to carry on when they can't. You'll never accept me as a mother but as your family, I want you to live. I want you to live."

"Mama, look," you shriek as you run into her room. "Look what Aunt Samira gave me."

You display the red bills into the air. Mama holds a finger to her lips and gestures toward the crib. You pounce onto the bed and land in her lap. "Can we go to the store? Can we? Can we?"

She chuckles. "Not now. Maybe some other day."

You pout. "But why?"

"Mama is very tired right now and Baba is at work."

You cross your arms. "I want a toy."

Mama sighs. "Some other day."

"I'll take him," Aunt says. She leans against the doorframe. "I'm not doing anything so I don't mind."

Mama shakes her head. "No, it's okay, Samira. He can wait."

You whip your head toward your mother. "Please?"

Mama looks at Aunt and pauses, holding her gaze until she nods. You shriek.

"Shhh," Mama says.

You slap a hand over your mouth and dash out of the room. "Let'sgoLet'sgoLet'sgo."

Aunt bends down to tie your shoelaces. You slip your hand into hers.

The back of your eyes sting and your heart buries itself deep into your stomach. It squeezes, sending surges of pain throughout your limbs.

"Yusuf, what's wrong?"

You crack open your wet fingers to find Aunt Samira's soft eyes gazing at you. Your mouth opens wide as the wails you had suppressed escape.

She hugs you, rubbing your back. "Why are you crying?"

"I tripped and-and-I hurt my knee."

"Here, let me see."

She examines your torn pants and blows on the cut. "Is it better now?"

You shake your head. A slow grin spreads on her face. "How about...now?"

Her hands crawl all over you, laughter erupting from your throat. "Stop, stop, stop," you shriek as tears run down your face.

Her hands hover over your stomach. "Hmm, are you feeling better?"

You smile and duck underneath her. "No."

Your breathing speeds up.

"Aunt Samira," you scream as you jump into her arms.

She ruffles her hair. "You've gotten bigger." She bends down and lifts Mahmoud up with you. "And Mahmoud too."

Baba places a hand on her shoulder. "Where's Zayd?"

She looks over her shoulder. "He should be in the bathroom. Now, who's hungry?"

"Me," you shriek.

"Me too," Mahmoud cries.

Aunt laughs. "I made both of your favorites: Manakish and Fattoush."

You squeeze her neck. "Okay, okay. You don't want me to die right now, do you?" she coughs.

Aunt's voice drags you out of your daydream. "I've never asked you to do anything but please, promise me one thing. Just one thing. Please live. Please live, even if you have to force yourself to." She sniffles. "I just want you to live."

You shake your head. "No. No," you whisper.

Aunt lifts her head from her hands.

"No, no, *no.*" The words get louder.

Aunt crawls toward you and wraps an arm around you. Her voice is sharp. "What's wrong? What's wrong?"

You push yourself away from her, shaking your head. "Don't do this to me. Don't. Don't."

You inhale sharply. She shakes her head. "Don't do what?"

You pull yourself away, holding your hands up. "Stop. Stop. Stop talking."

"What's wrong?" she pleads. Her fingers grip your arm. You pry them off.

"Stop doing this." You exhale sharply. "Stop making me want to live. Stop making me want to live."

laila

BANG.

I turn onto my shoulder, my mind floating out of my dreams.

Bang.

My eyes jerk open. The ceiling grows crisp above me, a gentle stream of dust flowing down from above. My spine remains glued to the floor.

Bang.

I shoot straight up. Amir shifts a bit, propping himself up on his elbow. His eyes dart left and right. "What's wron—"

BANG.

I flinch, my arm colliding with the wall. His eyes widen. "What's that?" he whispers.

"I don't know."

Amir stands up. "We have to hide." He grips onto my arm and pulls me toward the back door.

Click.

We shuffle out and Amir slams the door behind us. "Over there," he points to three barrels.

Voices echo through the silent city, the *bangs* hushed now. "Open up," a man booms.

Amir shoves me behind the barrels and dives in with me. The breeze carries the whispers from the house next door.

BANG.

I jump, slamming into the fence. Amir rests his hand on my shoulder, pushing me toward the ground.

BANG.

I tilt my head toward Amir's ear. "Are they at our door?"

He doesn't answer.

BANG.

"Open the door or else we're coming inside," the man's voice thunders.

Silence.

"We're coming in," the voice announces.

BANG. CRASH.

Wood splinters into a million pieces. The crackle of each shard echoes in my ears. Boots thunder into our house, the *thuds* bouncing off every wall. I glue my body to the fence, burying my face into my knees. The rustling grows louder and louder, the boots like hornets swarming to attack.

Crack.

The back door slams open. My heartbeat drums in my ears, matching the footsteps creeping closer and closer. A shadow of a boot falls beside me and I pull my legs closer to my chest. "This place looks abandoned."

"Of course they've run. What else do you expect?"

Run? Run from who? My eyes dart toward Amir, whose eyebrows are furrowed. He shakes his head ever so slightly.

The voices retreat inside. "There's no point in wasting time here. We have other things to do."

Slam.

The doors lock shut. After a couple of heartbeats, Amir inches his head upward. I jerk him back down. "What are you doing?" I whisper with clenched teeth.

"What do you think? Checking if they're still here."

"Not now."

"Okay, okay." I release my hand that's clamped over his and he scoots toward the fence. I squeeze the tips of my fingers.

One,   two,   three,   four,   five, six...three-hundred-two, three-hundred-three—

"Can I check now?" Amir whispers. I turn my head, eyes focused on the sliver of the back door I can see. I nod. He inches his head over the barrel before turning toward me.

"I think—" he starts.

"Shh, be quiet."

"I think we're clear."

I shake my head. "Not yet. We should wait in case they come back."

Amir opens his mouth but closes it after a split second. He nods, slouching against the fence and stretching his legs.

"If you say so," he mutters right before leaning his head to the left and closing his eyes. Within a couple minutes, his mouth is cracked open, soft snores erupting from his throat.

I gawk at him. How can he be so relaxed? We were just attacked. Soldiers broke into our home. And he's sleeping?

I let out a frustrated sigh and glance down at my white knuckles still gripping my legs. Four fingers and one stub, barely working together to keep my legs close to the rest of me.

"We'll have to cut it off," the doctor says. His stone eyes remain on Baba's bleached face.

"Wh-why?" he sputters.

"The infection is too deep. We can't wait for it to spread any longer."

Baba shoots straight out of the chair, his arm wrapping around my shoulders. "You can't do that. You made us wait for days for our turn and now, you're telling us it's too late?"

The doctor sighs. "It's not our fault. The hospital is overcrowded. We had more important cases to tend to."

Baba's voice grows loud. "And what could be more important than an infected finger?"

"Heart attacks, strokes, diabetes, cancer. The list goes on and on. But the choice is yours. Do you want her to lose one finger or her whole arm?"

Baba glances at me. "Can you put her to sleep before you do it?"

The doctor peers down at his clipboard. "We can't use anesthesia for this small of a procedure. They're reserved for major surgeries. I'm sorry."

Baba stiffens beside me. "So she'll feel the pain?"

My head jerks up, my mouth dry. The doctor nods. "I'm sorry. Unless you can pay for it, we can't give your daughter anesthesia."

The doctor turns to leave.

"How much?"

"Hm?"

"How much for anesthesia?" Baba asks.

"Fifty thousand liras."

Baba's mouth drops open, the whites of his teeth glimmering in the little light coming from the ceiling. "Wh-What?"

"That's why I didn't tell you the price earlier. I'll go prepare the equipment and then we'll move on to the procedure."

The doctor disappears behind a corner. I peer up at Baba. "I'm scared," I whisper.

He crouches down, his heavy eyes meeting mine. "Don't be afraid."

"Will it hurt?" I ask.

He shakes his head but his mouth curls into a frown and his eyes grow heavy.

"Are you lying?"

Baba pulls me into a hug. "Why would I lie to you?"

"Do you promise?"

Baba freezes for a split second. "I'll be with you the whole time."

"You didn't answer the question," I murmur. "It's going to hurt."

The doctor comes into view in the hallway, flanked by a nurse holding a blue basket. He nods when he sees me watching. The nurse places the basket on the bed. My eyes catch the knife inside.

"No, no," I shriek, pushing myself off the bed. Baba catches me.

"Shhh, it'll be okay."

The doctor reaches for Baba's shoulder and brings his mouth near his ear. Baba nods. His hands grip onto my arm.

"I'm sorry," he whispers.

I thrash in his grip, kicking my feet. The nurse holds onto my ankles while Baba pins my wrists. The doctor sits on a chair, snapping his gloves and mask on.

"No. No. No."

samira

A *CRACK* ESCAPES the door as it slides open. Light floods into the darkness, reaching every corner. My eyes burn and I cover them. Footsteps swarm around the car, the *thuds* growing louder as they inch closer.

An iron hand latches onto my arm, tearing me from the shadows. The white light blurs everything into green and brown blobs. I blink a couple of times, the fuzz morphing into reality.

A building, painted with shades of gray and black, lies ahead of me. It's one story but makes up for its height with its length. Its doors almost completely camouflage into its walls and the pipes circling it are tinged orange and brown. Around the facility, metal shines in the light, wires woven tightly between the bars. Dangling in front is a greasy sign.

Sini Detention Center.

I shudder and twist my wrists. They refuse to budge just like every other time. Yusuf steps out of the vehicle. His eyes are red and raw, damp streaks running down his cheeks. The soldier behind me shoves him forward. "We go that way."

The soldier gripping my forearm tugs me in the opposite direction. I open my mouth, words barely forming in my throat. "But aren't we supposed to stay together? Since we're family."

He shakes his head. "No."

"But you can't separate us—"

"We *can* separate you. We can do whatever we want."

The grains of sand rub against the rip in my shoe. "Who gave you permission? God?"

The man pinches the bridge of his nose. "Look, lady. I don't have time to argue with you. Rules are rules. End of story. Now, I would suggest you follow directions before I lose my patience."

"You didn't answer my question. If God didn't give you permission, then you can't do this. There are rules to war and—"

Crack.

My head jerks to the right, a blinding pain radiating from my skull. My hands skid against the sand.

"I told you not to provoke me."

I move my jaw side to side, my head growing numb. A hand lifts me off the ground, pulling me away from Yusuf.

The man's words slur into a garbled mess. "Now, if thar re o poblems, you'll flollow ornders."

My head throbs, the pounding echoing in my ears. "Huh?"

I look up, trying to make out Yusuf but a white pain flashes through my head as soon as I move my neck. I swallow my yelp.

.   .   .

The soldier lets go once we're deep inside the building. The hallways close in with every step. The walls sway, the flickering lights dancing in front of me as if warning me.

Go away. Go away. Go away.

I glance toward one of the soldiers, eyes catching on the hand resting on his pistol. It's too close. One shot and I'm dead.

Click.

A hand pushes me inside and then my shoulder is cold from where the grip left. The ground trembles beneath my feet. My arms flail, wrapping around cold metal.

A sharp inhale echoes from below and something slips out from under my foot. I slide against a boiling wall until my fingers brush the wet floor.

The room is still spinning left and right when a putrid smell slaps my nose. It's as if sewer water has been thrown in here. I clap a hand to my mouth, whimpering as the bile climbs my throat.

Whirling, monstrous figures settle in my vision, my eyes tracing each one. Their eyes are glued to me while their bodies are pressed to the wall.

"Another person? Why did they put another person in here?" a woman asks, her voice rising.

"We can barely breathe with forty people already. We can't be sharing the little air we have with another person," another one whispers.

I open my dry lips. "I'm sorry," I mutter. "I'm really sorry."

A blanket of silence descends on them. None of them utters a single word. I lick my lips and my mouth instantly fills with acid.

"Mmm. Mmm," I cry, pointing at my mouth.

Everyone scrambles and my cheeks burn.

"Here. Here." My fingers wrap around a metal container and I shove my face into it. The sewage smell explodes in my face and I open my mouth. More and more acid climbs out of my stomach, stinging my tongue.

The other women clamor toward the walls as I continue to puke. After a couple minutes, I place the bucket next to me and squeeze my head. My fingers come back slick and wet.

yusuf

YOUR FEET BURY themselves into the sand as you watch the soldier drag Aunt away. A hand pulls on your handcuffs and you lurch to the side. The soldier near you pulls you behind him.

Your feet skid against the sand and you're shaking your head vigorously. The soldier tugs. The force sends you crashing into the sand.

"You can stay right there if you want to. I'll make sure your eyes are open when I slit your mother's neck."

You peer over your shoulder at Aunt, a stream of blood dripping down her face and her limp body flailing in the sand. You open your mouth to call out to her but your tongue is still frozen in place.

.   .   .

The lightbulbs flicker above your head, illuminating the red-stained walls and damp floor. Each time they grow dark, a faint shadow creeps closer toward you but retreats as soon as the lights return. The handcuffs around your wrists hug them, carving purple-red valleys into your skin. Every so often, the soldier behind you shoves you forward. The pain from the impact reminds you that you're still a mortal in the world.

"Are you going to kill me?" you croak.

The guard scoffs. "Who do you think you are? The president of Syria to be asking such *princely* questions? Death is the easy way out and here, there's no easy way."

"Are you eventually going to kill me?"

He cackles. "The audacity of this boy." Voices deep in the hall laugh. "You want to die so bad, boy? Is that what you want? It's because you know too much, right? Now your mission is to find a rope or knife to take your life. Is that how precious your bosses are to you that you'd kill yourself for them?" A hand pinches the muscle surrounding your shoulder. "We'll see how you handle what we're going to give you. Let me clarify—the *gifts* we're going to give to you, your majesty."

His mouth moves toward your ear. "I have a question for you. Are you a king?"

You shake your head. The guard slaps you on the back, his mouth erupting with laughter. "I haven't had this much fun in ages. It will be such a pleasure dealing with you."

To your right, square holes appear from the walls. With every step you take, a white ball cracks open, following your every movement.

laila

AS THE SUN ascends from its bed, the sounds of Douma return: the *crrr* of crickets, the *wrrr* of the wind, the *scrrr* of trash slamming into houses. My head is limp to the right, my eyes barely cracked open. Dread settles in my stomach. If I don't open my eyes, nothing exists. If nothing exists, then we aren't alive. If we aren't alive, then there's no war.

But the erupting sunlight pries my eyelids wide open. Everything mashes into each other, the sky and the dirt bleeding. Amir is drawing in the dirt beside me, the twitching of his finger matching my slow heartbeat.

"I think we can go inside now. There hasn't been a single sound from the house in hours," he says, standing up. I grip onto a barrel and pull myself off the ground, my legs bent at awkward angles because of my tight muscles. I shake them and stretch, blood finally warming my limbs.

Amir grips the door handle, pausing for a couple seconds. He glances over his shoulder with a questioning look. "See, there's nothing to be afraid of."

Click.

The door slides to the left. My breath hitches while Amir gasps beside me. I dig my nails into my palm.

Inside, the little we have is thrown all across the floor. The mattresses are woven together, bootprints painted all over them. The walls cave in some places while the plastic sheet covering the ceiling has a deep gash, sunlight penetrating the cut. Our three cups twirl on the floor, one of them cracked across the top.

"Let's clean this up," Amir mutters.

I sink my knees into the mattress pile and slide each one out of the other. My eyes grow heavy. Amir is in the other corner, placing the cups on the counter. I snake my hand deep through the pile.

"Ow," I yelp.

I stare at the red dot spreading on my finger and stuff it into my mouth. A shadow darkens the floor in front of me. My eyes land on the pool of glass.

Amir squats next to me. "I'll clean this up."

"It's just a little cut. I can handle it. Go clean something else."

Amir hardens himself as I push against him. "Please. I want to finish this," I whisper. I want to piece back the little we have.

He stares at me for a while before hauling himself away. I reach into the river of glass and fish out a picture. My fingers graze the glossy paper, landing on Mama's face. My eyes fix on the black line streaming down the frame.

"Ahmed." Mama bursts through the door. Baba steps from behind the counter. "Look."

Mama holds out a golden necklace. "It broke."

Baba examines the separate chains. "Did the locket break too?"

Mama shakes her head and opens her other hand. Inside is an open locket, the two circles glinting in the sunlight. On the left is a picture of Baba at their wedding, fitted in a black suit. On the right I hold baby Amir, my fingers lightly brushing his hair.

Baba's eyes return to the chain in his hands. "I'll fix this after work. For now, keep it on the counter."

Amir's cries erupt from a room and Mama dashes toward it. Baba slips his shoes on. He holds his arms out. I run into them and he pecks my head. "I'm going to work now."

"Okay, Baba."

He puts me down and closes the door behind him. Amir's cries die down a bit. I climb onto the counter, my fingers curling around the icy chain.

I gasp under my breath. Each link in the chain glistens in the light, the twinkle transferring to my eyes. I wrap the necklace around my wrist.

A girl's voice rings from behind the front door. "Laila. Laila."

I hop off the counter, necklace in hand. I turn the doorknob. Our neighbor, seated on a pink bicycle, waves at me. "Let's play."

I rub the chain in my hand. "What's that?" the girl asks.

"A necklace."

The girl's eyes light up. "Can I see?"

I glance down at my clenched hand, before giving it to her. She grins, two holes in her smile. "Can I wear it for five minutes?"

I bite my lip and shake my head.

"Please?"

"I don't know."

"Pleeeeeeaseeeeeeeeee."

"Fine."

The girl jumps up from her bike. "Thankyouthankyouthankyou. Now let's go."

I jump onto my bike. I strap my helmet under my chin. "Hurry up," the girl cries.

"Coming."

As soon as I'm out from behind the fence, the girl takes off. I pedal toward her, a sheen of sweat spreading across my back. The wind carries our chuckles.

And then, the girl digs her heels into the dirt. She jerks forward, knuckles gripping onto her handlebars. I skid beside her. She turns to me with widened eyes. "It broke."

I cock my head to the side. "What broke?"

"The necklace."

My jaw drops. "Wh-What?"

"It flew off while I was riding...and I accidentally drove over it."

My head snaps side to side as my eyes take in every little sparkle on the ground. I curl my hands into fists. Anger seeps through my veins. "You what?"

The girl cowers. "I'm sorry. I'm really sorry."

"It was Mama's favorite" I toss my bike to the ground and rush toward the specks of gold. I lay a couple in my hand but after a few seconds, the breeze scatters them all over again. I grab what I can before pedaling madly down the street. "I'm sorry," the girl calls out but my eyes remain glued to our front door as it draws closer and closer. I toss my bike in the alley and duck inside the house.

"Laila?" Mama calls out. I freeze.

"Yes?"

She appears from inside the bathroom. "Where were you?"

"Outside."

Mama nods. "Do you want to help me make dinner?"

"Okay."

Mama smiles and heads over to the kitchen, her hand brushing the counter. She freezes. "You haven't seen my necklace by any chance, have you?"

I shake my head, rubbing the few chain links I could salvage behind my back. "That's strange. Ahmed told me he would leave it here...I guess he took it with him."

I climb onto the counter near the stove and watch as she reaches for a knife. My stomach bubbles until it's almost in my mouth.

"Mama?"

"Hm?"

"I know where your necklace is," I whisper.

She turns around, her eyes soft. I hold out the bits of gold in my hand. A fat tear drips down toward the ground. "It was an accident...I'm sorry."

Mama crouches in front of me. "That's why you need to ask before you take someone's things. If you would have asked me, I would have said yes. Now, why did you lie?"

I sniffle. "Because you'd get mad."

"Am I mad right now?" I glance up at her face and I shake my head. "See, that's why you're not supposed to lie. It would have been much easier for you to tell the truth right away. Do you promise you won't lie again?"

I nod vigorously. "I'm sorry Mama. I won't do it again."

She smiles and she holds out the locket with our pictures in it. "It's okay. I have the most important part right here."

samira

I SLIDE MYSELF into a centimeter-long space between two women, resting my head on my arm. The woman beside me murmurs under her breath and glues her body to the wall. My lungs, throat and tongue are hot, searing my insides. Every breath is laborious. I have to swallow back vomit with every inhale of the putrid air.

The pounding in my arm echoes inside my ear and the side of my head still tingles. I brush my fingers against my hijab. It's crusty and hard. I scratch it but the pain burns into my eyes, everything bursting into flashes of white.

*   .   .   .*

BEEP. BEEP. BEEP. BEEP.

I shoot upward. My vision blurs with black spots dancing in front of me. My head is heavy, tilting toward the ground. I blink a couple of times as a million blobs shift.

Something squeezes my ankle. "Ow," I shriek, curling myself into a ball.

"Out of the way," a thin voice responds.

Then, a stampede starts. Thousands of legs shade the ceiling, like encroaching storm clouds. They slam into my back, legs, neck, everywhere. I wrap my arms around my head, thrashing against the crowd.

And then, it dies down.

The thundering retreats down the hallway. The cell doors rock gently against a wall. The yellow of the lightbulbs is stable now, the glow reflecting off the black, tiled floor.

Raspy breathing rings in my ears as the footsteps fade into soft whispers. I turn to my right to find a woman slumped in the corner. Her head hands low, tiny droplets falling off her chin. Her eyes are barely cracked open, red lines snaking through them.

I rest my back against a wall, unable to hold myself up any longer. The woman's head lifts every so slightly and her heavy eyes find mine. A worn smile spreads on her face.

"You should go. This is the only meal you'll get today," she croaks.

"What about you?" I mutter, barely hearing my own voice.

She sighs. "There's no point. The food can never stay down."

"I'm-I'm sorry."

She shakes her head. "Don't be." A cough rattles through her body and she brings her twig fingers up to cover her mouth. "Don't be sorry."

Her head falls back again.

I grip onto the boiling metal bars and pull myself off the ground. My legs wobble, my knees trembling with my weight. I take one step at a time until the cell is just a shadow behind me. The white in the halls stings my eyes as my hand brushes against the walls. Soon, the echo of clattering rings from the end of the narrow passage.

I peek from behind the wall. The hallway opens to a wide room with stained white walls. The ceilings are low, my head almost touching the top. To the right, women huddle on the floor, their hands shoving goop into their mouths. A few feet from them, a line of women snakes, each person holding a cracked, brown plate in their hands.

My stomach hisses, forcing me into the line.

Four people.

Three people.

Two people.

One person.

Me.

I hold out my plate. The man behind the counter glares at me with empty eyes. "We ran out."

I cock my head to the side, peering at the half-full bucket in front of him. "But there's food right there."

He grimaces. "I don't think you heard me. We ran out."

I furrow my eyebrows and point toward the bucket. "There's some righ—"

Clank.

The man smashes his ladle against the counter, his eyes narrow. The little clatter of spoons fades into complete silence. *"There's no food."*

Heat pricks my face. My stomach growls, staring at the brown mush in the bucket. My lips are sticky and cracked. I lick at them. "Can I at least have—"

The man's mouth bends into a scowl. "Guards," he calls out.

I step back, hugging the plate to my chest. A man dressed in gray walks into the room. The women on the floor inch closer to each other, their eyes trained on their plates and nothing else. The man behind the counter says something to the guard, his finger pointed at me.

My heart cracks my ribcage. The soldier turns toward me, his hands resting on his belt. A whimper escapes my throat.

He bends so that his eyes are at my level. "I don't think you understood his words so let me clarify. It doesn't matter what you see. When one of us says something, you listen. That's it. And if you don't—" the man pats his pistol. "Well, you know what happens."

yusuf

CLICK.

You crack open your eyes, following the figure stomping through the cell door. Within a second, the room is engulfed in blinding, white light. You clap your hands over your face.

The other prisoners clamor toward the walls, parting for the man. You reach for the wall until each vertebrae in your back squeezes against it. A hand grips the back of your shirt.

"Get up," a voice rings.

A hand pulls you to your feet, your eyes still burning from the light. You glance over your shoulder at the other prisoners. Their eyes are laced with horror, the blacks of their eyes only tiny dots now.

The men push you out of the cell and your heart begins to race.

Thump.

Thump.

Thump.

The halls are lifeless, only the rumble of boots echoing. The shadow of the hallway succumbs into a deeper black in the shape of a door.

Your feet halt.

A hand pinches your shoulder. "I wouldn't do that if I were you," a voice whispers in your ear.

But your feet refuse to obey. Suddenly, the air is knocked out of your lungs and you trip forward, face skidding against the boiling tile. Without warning, hands swarm around you, tossing you onto a chair. Cool metal bites into your wrists and ankles. A light switches on above you.

A man, short yet muscular, emerges from the shadows. He laces his fingers together behind his back and paces back and forth in front of you. "I'll explain this to you in an easy manner. It's not that difficult to understand. I ask the questions, you give the answers. Make sense?"

You hang your head low. A gust of air brushes against you and the man crouches. His hands swat your hair away but you keep your eyes fixed on a spot on the ground.

And then his face is all you can see. His chin is sharp while his nose shoots straight out of his skin. His lips are twisted into a smile. It's just a mask for what's in his eyes though. They're a piercing gray but if you look hard enough, you can see a subtle glint of red.

"Let me repeat myself. You answer the questions I ask you. Do you understand?"

You nod ever so slightly. The soldier stands up. "We'll start with a very basic question. What's your name?"

"Yusuf," you whisper.

The man sighs loudly. "Tsk, tsk. When someone asks for your name, you give them your *full* name. Your *full* name. I'll give you another chance. What's your name?"

"Yusuf Salah."

"Good, good. Just what I want to hear. Where were you born?"

"Raqqa."

"And how old are you?"

"Eighteen," you croak.

"Ah, eighteen. A bittersweet age when you're at the brink of adulthood but still a child. Now, tell me. What happens when someone turns eighteen?"

You shrug your shoulders.

"You don't know, Mr. Salah?"

"No."

"I'll tell you then. You're old enough to work for ISIS. That's what happens when you turn eighteen."

You shake your head.

"No, that's not true? Are you calling me a *liar?*"

You shake your head.

"Then what do you mean?"

You crack open your mouth to speak. "I've never worked for them," you mutter.

"But I never asked that. I never asked if you worked for them, just that you're old enough to." You can hear the smirk in the man's voice.

"I'll ask another question, the question you were so eager to answer. Do you work for ISIS?"

"No."

"Where are all your words now?" the man asks. He pauses for a moment. "I can see that you don't talk much but for this to be a conversation, you need to use that mouth of yours. I can't be the only person talking."

You nod. "Good, good. You said that you don't work for ISIS, right? Alright then, you're free to go."

Your head jerks upward and you lock eyes with the soldier. His mouth curls into a grin. "Just kidding. I would never let you go that easily."

Your lungs tighten and our breathing rings in your ears.

"Now, now. No need to be afraid. We're friends after all. Nevermind, we're not friends. You're trying to kill me."

Your jaw drops. The man shakes his head. "Don't act so surprised. Do you think I'm an idiot?"

"No, I—" you begin but he cuts you off.

"I'm still talking," he sings. He inches his face toward yours. "ISIS sent you here to wreak havoc and you're obviously going to follow their orders. Now, since that plan of yours has been foiled, you need to escape. The only way you can escape is by killing me. It's simple, really."

"No," you mutter.

"Then what? What assignment has ISIS given you?"

"They haven't given me anything."

"You're just making this more difficult for yourself. Just tell me what they told you and I'll let you go, simple as that."

Your voice trembles. "I'm not working for them."

"Shaky voice. Classic sign of lying. Check." He makes a checkmark in the air.

You shake your head.

"Denying. Another sign." The soldier jumps up with excitement. He clears his throat. "Anyway, it doesn't matter how much you deny this. It's my

duty to ensure Syria is safe. Safe from people like
you."

laila

MY STOMACH SHRIEKS, folding inward. Amir crouches beside me, plucking the picture from my hands and brushing the shards of glass away. "Let's go find something to eat," he says.

I nod but my legs refuse to straighten. Amir tugs on my hand. "Come on. I'm hungry," he whines.

As soon as I stand up, he shoves me out the door, the house trembling as he slams the charred wood. Soon, the soothing *krr krr* of his footsteps rings in front of me. He clears his throat. "Why are you slow? Aren't you hungry?"

My eyes remain fixed on his. He sighs. "Look, I know you're upset but you can't just sit there, expecting food and water to fall from the sky. We need to do something and I can't be the only one doing it."

My tongue sinks into my mouth, refusing to budge. A prick of rage injects itself into my blood, conquering the heaviness in my heart. Amir glances over his shoulder. "Are you going to respond?"

I clench my teeth. He shrugs his shoulders. "You can sulk all you want. I'm going to get food, whether you want to or not."

Heat spreads across my face, the muscles in my jaw tensing.

"Seems like only one of us is grieving Baba."

Amir freezes mid-step and whips around toward me. "What?"

"It seems like only one of us is actually grieving Baba."

Amir's face drains and his pupils dilate to little black dots in a sea of green and white. He clenches his fists and stomps deeper into the street.

A pang of guilt pulses through my limbs. I'm the older sister. I shouldn't be like this. I should be there for him, not the other way around. I reach out for his shoulder. "Don't even think about it," he snarls.

"I'm sorry," I whisper.

He scoffs, his mouth curling from the sides, and his pace quickens. He makes a sharp turn into the baker's shop. A middle-aged man smiles at us, his eyes bloodshot. His beard is overgrown in patches, gray tinging the ends of his hair. "How may I help you?" he asks, his voice soft.

Amir swallows. "We-we don't have money."

The light in the backer's eyes vanishes. Amir opens his mouth again. "We have nothing to eat and our father...he isn't here anymore. It's embarrassing to ask but could you please spare a loaf?"

The baker shakes his head. "I'm sorry. I've already given out six free loaves. I can't afford to keep giving. I need the money too."

Amir clasps his hands together and holds them in front of the backer. "Please?"

He shakes his head again.

"But then, we'll starve to death."

The baker's eyes jerk toward Amir. "You're not the only ones who could starve to death," he snaps, "I have a family too. I have children who rely on me, who need to eat. I *can't* give you bread for free."

Amir's eyes glisten. "Please," he whispers.

The baker shakes his head vigorously. "I'm going to have to ask you to leave so I can serve other customers."

Amir spins on his heels and thunders out of the shop doors, his head hanging down toward the dirt. I grip his wrist. Amir's a kid. He shouldn't have to lose hope too. "We can try other stalls. Maybe the butcher is willing to give us something like fat or bones he wants to throw away."

Amir twists his arm out of my grasp. "So now you want to be proactive? Now you want to act like a real older sister?"

I suck in air through the small gap between my teeth. "I'm grieving Baba too," he snaps, "I miss him. I miss Mama. But they would want us to keep living. For the both of us, to keep living."

"I'm sorry," I mutter.

He nods, a sigh escaping his lips. "The butcher *sells* his bones. We can't afford that. and there are going to be too many kids looking for food in the dump. Let's go check the trenches. Someone could have thrown their scraps there."

Amir takes off across the street and I stay a couple of steps behind him. The bubble of conversation from the market dies down the farther we travel. Soon, a sea of sand takes over, yellow reflecting every ray of sunlight. Amir's head darts left and right and he skids down the side of the trench.

Inside, helmets and bullet shells are scattered on the black dirt, signs of a war we so desperately try to forget. Coils of barbed wire peek from the dirt wall surrounding the trench, warning us not to touch them. I glance down at the hole in my shoe, at my toe rubbing against the ground.

A whimper echoes a couple of steps away from me. My head jerks upward, my eyes landing on Amir.

I take a step toward him. "What's wr—"

I freeze when I see it too. Baba's briefcase and shoes.

samira

THE GUARD TURNS back toward the gray hall, nodding at the kitchen man as he leaves. The gentle ring of spoons and plates fills the air again. But all the other women stay in the same position, their eyes focused on the table and their mouths chewing robotically.

My hand is slick now, my plate threatening to slip out from my fingers. I place it down on a stack of dirty dishes near the counter and duck into the hallway. As I travel further, the sounds from the cafeteria drown into silence.

I pause to look at the tunneling hallway. It twists and turns, running from the light. On the right wall are countless doors, all of them black and bolted. I drag my hand against it, my nails rubbing against the cracks.

I rest my fingers on one of them and press on the handle.

Locked.

I try another one.

Locked.

Another.

Locked.

Locked.

Locked.

Slam.

I clap a hand over my mouth.

Slam.

I stumble away from the door.

Slam.

The door creaks with the pressure. The nails holding it groan.

Rap. Rap. Rap.

"Is someone there?" a girl's low and strained voice cries. "Hello? Is someone there? Can you help?"

My heart batters against my ribs. I pull on the door handle but it refuses to move more than a millimeter.

"Please help me."

A lump in my throat blocks any sound from coming out. The girl bangs on the door again. "Please," she hiccups.

"I can't," I whisper but the words are so quiet, I can barely hear them.

SLAM. SLAM. SLAM.

I jerk away from the door, my back sinking into the cell bars behind me. The sounds echo throughout the hall.

BANG. BANg. BAng. Bang. bang.

I stumble as far as I can, squeezing my face with my fingers. My ears throb, just as loud as that imprisoned girl. I duck behind a wall, gripping onto it with white fingers.

Heavy footsteps inch close and a fist pounds on a door. "Shut up," someone growls.

The girl inside the cell goes quiet. My heart sputters, sparing my ribs from the constant pressure. I inhale deeply.

Yusuf. He must be in here somewhere.

I force my feet forward and slide against the wall. In front of me, countless cell doors lie open with an occasional sick or elderly woman slumped against a cell.

I reach a dead end and turn left. Pipes snake along the ceiling and the vents above them hiss frequently. There are only a few doors but as my fingers brush against each handle, they barely move.

Creeeeak.

I jerk backward, my eyes fixed on the expanse before me. I take a few steps back and look left and right but there are no turns or hallways, just a door.

I tug on the handle but it refuses to budge.

Creeeak.

I whimper, pulling harder on the handle. I dig my heels against the wall and lean backward but all the door does is chuckle softly.

Crash.

My hand slips and I tumble into the pipes behind me. The broiling metal sears my skin, a flash of white pain radiating from my back. A yelp escapes my mouth.

I pull myself up and reach for the handle again. As soon as I do, something heavy lands on my shoulder. My muscles freeze.

"What do you think you're doing?"

yusuf

YOUR HEART DROPS. "I have nothing to do with ISIS."

The man scoffs. "Alright. Let's say I believe you for the next minute. How will you prove your innocence to me?"

"I don't have a weapon." You lift your wrist just a millimeter but the metal bites into your skin.

"That doesn't counter the fact that you have instructions from ISIS regarding where to attack and when. How you do it is up to you. You don't need weapons if you so choose."

You shake your head.

"Prove it to me."

"Please live." Aunt Samira's voice rings in your head. *"I just want you to live."* Tears prick your eyes. The commander leans toward you. "You have no proof, do you?"

Your throat closes tight, air barely entering. Your stomach twists into a knot and squeezes.

"Since you can't prove your innocence, you're guilty. I won't stop until you give me every detail I can juice out of your brain. What did ISIS tell you to do?"

"Nothing," you croak.

The man pinches the bridge of his nose and sighs. "This could have been so easy, if only you would listen." He stands up and turns toward the guards that have been swarming around him for the past hour. "You know what to do," the commander gruffs and slams the door behind him.

The light clicks off. The cuffs digging into your ankles and wrists slide open and a hand pushes you to the floor.

And then nothing.

You crack your eyes open and lift your head an inch off the ground.

Thud.

You recoil. Air floods out of your lungs.

Thud.

Bile clamps in your throat and you cough. You pull your knees up to protect your stomach.

Thud. Thud. Thud.

Pain flashes everywhere. The boots come from every direction, disguised in the darkness.

It doesn't stop.

Thud. Thud. Thud.

The boots slam again and again.

Snap.

Something collides with your nose and a horrible, raw *crack* rings in your ears. You reach up but your hand flies back as a boot pins it back down.

Creeeak.

The kicks stop. You crack open your eyes. The black is everywhere and nowhere.

"Has he confessed?"

"No, sir," another voice responds.

Your curled body is lifted off the ground. "You're not going to give in, huh? This is *just* the beginning."

The man drops you and you bounce off the floor. The kicks continue. You wrap your arms around your head, making yourself as small as possible.

But they continue.

A metallic taste spreads in your mouth. Your chin is wet, rivers dripping from it.

Thud. Thud.

Your ribcage gives in, a deafening *crack* echoing in your ears.

Bzzzz. Bzzzzz.

"Pause for a minute," the man orders and the kicks stop. You lie on the ground, limp.

"Hello?" the man says. His voice is soft and quiet now, the complete opposite of what it was a few seconds ago.

A child's voice rings from the other end of the call. "Daddy, when will you come home?"

The soldier chuckles. "Soon, soon."

"When you come, can we eat ice cream?"

"Of course," he responds.

"Can I eat two scoops?" the child asks, his voice rising with excitement.

"You can eat as much as you want. I have to get back to work now, okay? I'll be home soon."

"Okay," the child sings and the line cuts.

laila

AMIR'S BREATH QUIVERS beside me. His fingers curl into fists, rocking against his legs rhythmically. My feet bury themselves into the ground, refusing to move.

"That's Baba's," he whispers, his voice raspy. "Why is it here?"

"I don't know," I respond.

"Why is it here?" he booms. I rest a hand on his shoulder, the *thump* of his heartbeat vibrating against my skin. His eyes are glassy as he turns to me.

"Maybe he lost it," I say.

Amir chuckles sadly. "You don't have to lie to me, you know? I'm not a child anymore. Why is his briefcase here? He wouldn't have gone to work without it."

"I don't know. I really don't," I whisper.

Amir's head tilts toward the sky and laughter breaks from his throat. My head snaps toward him, eyes focused on the smile on his face and the tears dripping down his cheek. He clenches his stomach. "Why is it here? Why?"

His words come out in desperate breaths. Amir's eyes meet mine and his smile vanishes.

I bend down to pick up the things but my fingers brush the bare earth. I cock my head and search the area. The briefcase and shoes are gone.

"Wha—"

I raise my head, meeting the gaze of the little boy hugging the items. His baggy clothes hang off his puny shoulders, holes and tears highlighting the bones hidden behind the cloth. His face is caked in dirt while his feet are bare, black and red cuts painted across his skin.

"Hey," Amir barks.

I furrow my forehead. "Don't yell at—"

But Amir brushes my words aside. He steps toward the child. "Give them back," he growls with clenched teeth.

The child shakes his head, arms wrapping tighter around the objects. I reach out. "May we have it back?" I ask, keeping my voice gentle.

The boy shakes his head and bends his legs. "No," Amir shrieks. The boy springs up, dashing deeper into the trench. I lurch forward, my hand barely holding onto Amir's shirt. Amir jerks backward, ripping himself away from me and disappearing into the black.

I chase after him. My lungs burn, my throat pleading for water while my muscles die from hunger. My stomach sinks deep into my abdomen. I stop and grip onto a dirt wall. My mouth hangs open, gulping in air.

Food. Food.

I drag myself across the trench, eyes combing the ground. But the ground has been stripped clean of every morsel. I slide to the dirt.

Thud. Thud. Thud.

Soft footsteps grow close. Amir trudges toward me, a coat of sweat shining on his face. My eyes wander to his hands, at the half slice of bread protected by his fingers.

I shoot straight off the ground. A smile tugs on Amir's mouth and he holds out half the bread. My fingers reach for it. It's rock hard and slightly blue from the edges.

I bring the piece near my nose and sniff a whiff of mold, flour and salt. I look up to see Amir's waiting eyes. I tear the bread into two parts and hold on out to him. Within a split second, our mouths are bulging. The crust cracks against my teeth, shards piercing the insides of my cheeks. As soon as I swallow, my stomach settles a bit.

"Thank you," I mutter. Amir nods, his mouth curling into a frown. I wrap my arms around him. "It's okay if that boy took our stuff," I say.

He shakes his head against my shoulder. "No, it's not. It's Baba's."

"But what if that boy really needs the money from selling it?"

"But what about us? *We* could sell it and buy food for *ourselves.*" Amir's tears catch onto my shirt, a cloud of black spreading across the cloth.

samira

THE SOLDIER RIPS me away from the door, dragging me behind him through the hallway. He tosses me into the cell, sliding his key into the lock.

I grip onto the bars, my breath shaky. My knees quiver until they can't hold me anymore. I collapse onto the floor and crawl toward a corner until my eyes catch on the sick woman from earlier. Her head hangs slightly to the left but her chest seems frozen. I inch closer and pull her hijab away from her eyes.

I jerk backward.

Her eyes are glassy and blank, staring right at me while her arms are limp, hanging beside her on the ground. My chest contracts, the pain traveling through my veins.

She's dead. She's dead.

I grip onto the cell door. "She's dead. She's dead. *She's dead,*" I scream.

Thud. Thud. Thud.

Three figures stomp into the hall. One of them kicks the bars, the vibrations rippling through my limbs. "Shut up," he snarls.

"She's dead," I murmur.

The soldiers' eyes dart behind me, to the woman's lifeless body. "You've never seen a dead body before?" one of them scoffs.

I take a shaky step backward, collapsing onto the floor. One of the soldiers glances to his side. "The others are coming," he announces and stands by the door as women step in without uttering a single word. One by one, each inch of space is occupied, except for a ring formed around the sick woman's corpse.

.   .   .

Creeeeeak. Thud. Thud.

My head snaps up, following the figure stepping into the cell. The other prisoners keep their heads low, their eyes barely cracked open. The soldier thunders around, eyes searching until he stops. He steps forward until he's right in front of a girl.

"Please, don't," she squeaks.

Crack.

The soldier strikes her across the face. A wail echoes throughout the cell.

"Make one more sound, I dare you," the soldier warns with clenched teeth. He pulls her off the ground and drags her out of the cell. Within seconds, her whimpers fade.

Gentle sobs ring in the cell. "My daughter. They took my daughter."

A woman wraps her arms around the grieving mother but the weeping rings even louder.

"Be quiet. They'll come back," another woman from the corner snaps.

"Reem is never coming back." The mother bangs her head against a wall. "I'll never see her again."

Thud. Thud.

"Be quiet."

The mother's eyes are lifeless and she continues slamming her head into the wall. "Reem. Reem. *Reem.*"

THUD. THUD.

Boots gallop closer and closer, like a stampede of horses. The door flings open and another soldier steps inside. The women shrink back, pressing themselves against the ground. My head sinks behind my knees so that only my eyes are visible.

Please leave, please leave, please leave.

"How many times are we going to have to come back here?" the man booms. I curl into myself.

"We deserve a reward for taking care of you, don't we?" He pauses. Silence settles in the cell and a sick smile spreads on his face.

He steps toward another young woman, his hand lifting her chin. Her breath quivers. The man twists a clump of hair underneath her hijab and drags her behind him. "My reward," he chuckles, his grin reaching his eyes.

As the girl stumbles out of the cell, she glances over her shoulder, her eyes wet and pleading.

But no one moves.

Click.

The door locks into place. I dig my fingers into the tile, squeezing my head between my knees. The thunder in my ears grows louder and louder.

Oh my God. Oh my God. Oh my God.

And it keeps getting worse. The pounding is everywhere now: my neck, my arms, my stomach.

Everywhere.

The cell wraps itself in silence again. The mother is still weeping into her hands. The sick woman's body rots in the corner, flies feeding off her flesh.

This is all a sick game. A game to fill our veins, to invade our every thought. In here, they have the weapons, the strength, the power. We have nothing.

A hand squeezes my arm. I crack open my eyes to see an older woman gazing at me with tender eyes and a faint smile. A red, oozing cut runs down her neck. "Don't worry. You'll get used to it."

yusuf

WHEN THEY STOP, you can't breathe. One of your eyes is swollen shut while something drips down the side of your mouth. Your stomach and chest are numb, your faint heartbeat throbbing in your temples.

"Get up," someone orders. You grip the floor and strain to lift yourself but you can only pull yourself an inch.

Crack.

You gag as another kick collides with your stomach. "Get up," the voice orders again.

"I-can't," you croak.

He scoffs. A hand grabs your shoulder and rips you off the ground. Your mind spins. The soldier lets you go and you fall backward against a wall. You hold onto your side, your head hanging limply.

"Look up."

You try but a white pain flashes through your neck and your head hangs to the left. A finger lifts your chin, pressing against a bruise. You clench your jaw. "When I tell you to do something, you do it. Understand?"

He lets go and your head snaps back. You squeeze your side, trying to subdue the throbbing.

"Are you ready to talk now—" the soldier asks.

"Move," the commander from earlier echoes. He squats, leaning so he can see your face.

"Now, after this little *adventure* of yours, you should know what I'm going to ask. All you have to do is nod. Simple as that. Are you working for ISIS?"

Your throat itches as your voice scratches against it. "No."

The commander shakes his head. "I gave you a chance. I tried but I can't help you if you won't help me. That's how a transaction works."

He stands up. "Bring them in," he says.

Creeeak.

Boots shuffle into the room. Scattered among the black are three pairs of bruised, bare feet. The commander squats down again and holds you head up with his hand, his fingers squeezing your cheeks.

"Look at them." Your eyes dart behind the commander's shoulder, meeting the three prisoners. Their feet are sliced, red clawing up their legs. Black rings circle their sunken eyes and their hair is pulled out from random places, like burnt bushes.

"You have a choice. Either you tell me the truth," his eyes point toward the prisoners, "or these people will die. You wouldn't want that to happen, would you?"

The prisoners' shining eyes widen. "We haven't done anything. We've been nothing but good," one of them begs. He clasps his hands together. "Please, have mercy."

"That's not my call." The commander cocks his head at you. "What's your choice?"

You stare at the prisoners in silence. Your voice is heavy as it vibrates in your throat.

"I'll tell you," you whisper.

The commander smiles. "See, how hard was that?" He nods toward his men and they release the prisoners.

They crumple to their knees. "Thank you, thank you," they cry.

The commander turns toward you. "Now, who communicated with you in Raqqa?"

"Qasim Aslam."

"That's odd. I've never heard of a *Qasim Aslam.*"

"That was his name," you croak.

"What did he tell you to do?"

"To plant a bomb in Homs."

"Homs, huh? That's a very long walk. I would expect Aleppo or Manjib would be easier to target. Less chances of getting caught. Don't you agree?"

You turn your head to the side, stifling the groan of pain erupting from your throat. "Those are the orders they gave me."

"How were you supposed to build this bomb? You didn't have anything on you."

"There is someone there who would give me the supplies."

The commander cocks his head. "So let me get this straight. There is someone working for ISIS in Homs who would give you the materials to build a bomb?"

You nod.

"That must take a lot of training. How long did they spend teaching you all this?"

"A couple months."

"You must be a fast learner to learn so quickly."

You keep your eyes locked on a black line on the wall. Your hands hang near the ground, your fingers caressing a puddle underneath you.

The commander stands up, gestures a guard over and points toward you. A hand lifts your head until you are looking straight ahead. "But do you know what the problem is? I don't believe you."

BANG.

One of the prisoners crumples to the ground. A red pool spreads around him, clawing through his clothes. Your breath hitches in your throat and you press yourself deeper into the wall. The other prisoners scream and thrash away from the body.

"Akhi, akhi, spare us. Spare us."

The commander shakes his head.

"You had a chance but you didn't take it. What a shame. What a shame indeed."

Bang. Bang. Bang.

laila

AMIR STANDS ON the ledge of the trench. He gazes out at the sandy expanse. "We should go look for him," he mutters.

I stiffen beside him. He continues. "If his stuff is here, it's proof that he left town, right? He could be in Ghasulah or Mesraba." He turns toward me, gripping my shoulders. "We have to go look for him. We *have* to."

My throat goes dry. I gaze at Amir's desperate eyes and nod. I can't take his hope away from him. I can't be the reason he breaks.

He grins. "We can leave when the sun sets and we'll reach Mesraba by sunrise."

He turns and walks down the street. "Are you sure?" I call out.

"I hope so," he responds.

.　　.　　.

Once the sun bleeds into the sky, Amir and I set off. With every step, the moon climbs an inch higher.

One step, one inch.

Two steps, two inches.

Three steps, three inches.

My feet scrape the warm sand and even though a cool breeze rubs against my limbs, beads of sweat drip down my skin.

My sandals catch on a rock and a yelp slips from my mouth. I turn my foot over to see a deep gash running through my shoe, sand clinging to my exposed skin. A literal thread holds the two pieces together. Amir crouches down beside me.

"I'll be fine," I mutter, "We have to keep moving."

White blurs zip near the horizon. "That's the highway," Amir says, "Come on."

I try to ignore the pebbles scraping my feet as the bright fuzz morphs into cars. If I don't think about it, it's not there. My shoes are not broken. I can't feel the ground. All of it is just my imagination.

Soon, the waves of sand thin as the ground morphs from yellow to the gray of the highway. Amir points at a metal sign hanging on a pole. *Mesraba: 10 km.*

"Almost there," he huffs.

I lean forward, fingers gripping my knees. My throat is stripped dry and my saliva is thick, refusing to go down. My stomach twists and turns, giving up on screaming and threatening to climb up my throat. My muscles plead for a sip of water.

But there's none. There's nothing here but sand. I need to hold on for just a little longer. Just a little longer.

I inhale deeply, feeling the air steal the few drops of moisture from my body. Amir glances toward me. "Ready?" he asks.

I nod. After a couple more hours, when the stars sink onto the sky and the moon rests in its throne, black silhouettes jut out on the horizon. An occasional white square illuminates their walls while a couple of street lights dot the roads.

At least there's some life here. Even though Mesraba has the same debris, the same cracked houses, the same destruction, at least there's proof of life. At least the silence is kept at bay with the *whir* of cars and the flickering neon signs of shops.

Amir ducks behind the closest alley and slides to the ground. "We can start asking people if they've seen Baba tomorrow." His mouth spreads in a yawn. "I'm exhausted."

He pats the space next to him. I sit down and he rests his head against my shoulder. "Try to sleep, okay?"

I nod. A couple minutes later, his gentle snores rock the sky.

.   .   .

The sun is a crack on the horizon when my eyes flutter open. Strands of slick hair stick to my left cheek. I turn slightly. Amir is still asleep with his mouth hanging open, his hair glued to both of our faces. I tap his head. "Wake up," I whisper in his ear.

"Mmm," he groans.

"The sun's up. We need to hurry and leave."

"Just a couple more minutes," he mutters. Amir curls into himself, his snores resuming after a couple of seconds.

I nudge his head. "Come on. We'll be late."

He doesn't budge. I push his head off my shoulder and it jerks up. He massages his neck. "Why would you do that?" he asks.

"Because you weren't waking up."

I pull myself up to my feet and hold my hand out to Amir. He takes it, straightening himself.

I brush the brown stains on my shirt but faint scars bury themselves deep into the fabric.

My toe itches as dust from the road rubs against it. Ahead, shopkeepers unlock their doors and flick switches, the signs above their crowded shops buzzing to life. A whiff of raw meat wafts from the butcher's store while the baker displays his new goods out on tables. Farmers drag carts behind them with an assortment of green, orange, red and other bright colors.

Amir flags down one of them and holds out a picture. "Assalam Alaikum. Have you seen this person?"

The man eyes him suspiciously. "No." Then he turns around without a single care. Amir's eyes drop and he swallows hard. I need to distract him.

"What picture is that?" I ask Amir. He holds it out to me. Baba's eyes are barely open as a smile is spread wide across his face. His shoulders are the only other part of his body in the photo, covered by a black tuxedo.

"His wedding picture," I whisper.

Amir nods and steps into the bakery. He walks up to the counter. "Assalam Alaikum. Have you seen this man?"

The baker shakes his head. The cycle continues. I lurk behind Amir, my throat raw. With every 'no,' my heart sinks deeper and deeper into my intestines. My ears ring with confirmation of what I already knew. Baba isn't here. He's gone somewhere far away, either willingly or unwillingly. But he's definitely not in Masraba.

Amir slouches after another 'no.' "He's not here," he mutters. "I've asked over thirty people. No one has seen him."

"That's not enough." I glance up at the cloudless sky. "We still have time. Ask another thirty people."

He holds the picture up to his nose. "There's no point. He's not here. Let's just go home."

Amir trudges back down the street, his feet rubbing against the dirt, sending clouds of dust flying in the air.

samira

BEEP. BEEP. BEEP.

The walls vibrate against my back, jolting me awake. All the eyes in the cell snap open. The crying mother from last night remains still with her bloodshot eyes and glistening face.

Click.

The women inch toward the wall as a guard steps into the cell. "Stay still," he barks. "One, two, three, four, five, six…forty-five, forty-six, forty-seven. There are enough," he calls behind him.

"Bring them out," a distant voice responds.

"Let's go," the guard yells. The women stir quietly but none of them stands. "I said *let's go.*"

Everyone shoots straight off the floor. The soldier bangs his rifle against the cell door. "Move it."

The line inches out of the cell. In the hallway, the air is thinner and cooler but my clothes stick to my skin. "Where are we going?" someone whispers from the back.

"Are you talking?" a soldier growls. I sink my head a bit, hiding behind the woman in front of me. Up ahead, a door the size of a wall hangs over the back of a trunk. The line halts in front of the vehicle.

"Why are you stopping? *Get in.*"

The woman at the front of the line hesitates. "Where are we going?"

A soldier near her grumbles. "When I say get in, that means you get in without asking any questions." He shoves her shoulders and she stumbles into the truck. The line creeps forward.

As I step into the vehicle, I cough. The air inside the truck is hot and stale, threatening to suffocate me. The tires whines as the women settle.

"Is that all of them?"

"Yes."

And then, it's pitch black inside.

The truck screeches to a halt and I'm flung to the side. From the front of the vehicle, doors crack open and shut.

Creak.

The trunk doors are thrown open. I clap a hand over my eyes, the light blurring my vision.

"Out," someone barks and one by one, we tumble out of the shadows into the terrain of the sun. My feet rub against the boiling sand. The air outside is free, still stiff but fresh.

Krrrr.

I whip backward, right before the truck's tires begin to spin. The men inside don't even glance back toward us.

"Did they just leave?" someone asks. A gentle hum falls over the group as everyone begins to talk.

"I'm going home," someone declares and walks off.

"Me too."

"Same."

One by one, the group grows smaller and smaller until only four of us are left. "We should go too. Maybe look for a town and figure out where we are," a girl suggests.

We follow as she begins to walk in a random direction. I glance over my shoulder where the dull sand meets the sky. I weave my fingers together. The gray compound is nowhere in sight. I don't even know what direction we came from, let alone how to find my way back. How am I going to get back? How am I going to find Yusuf?

How am I going to protect him if I don't even know where he is?

.   .   .

"Are those...buildings?" One of the women points toward the horizon. Just where the sun descends into its slumber, a gray building stands erect.

"It is. It's a city." The women jump up and down, hugging each other. "Let's go."

A couple minutes later, the buildings grow crisp in the sunlight. Most of them are half-destroyed, exposing the tangle of pipes, furniture and cement inside. Newspapers and plastic bags soar in the air, replacing the birds that used to fly.

But what's most striking are the people standing on the outskirts. I squint and my blood freezes at the sight of sticks on their shoulders.

My vision begins to blur from the edges. We're in ISIS territory.

yusuf

THEY TOSS YOU into a cell. Your arms collide with the stone floor, your cuts and bruises igniting on fire. You dig your nails into the tiles, trying to pull yourself forward. But the other prisoners swarm away from you. The soldier scoffs and kicks you one last time.

Click.

You slide against the floor. A flashing pain erupts through your stomach and you yelp. The prisoners sink further into the wall.

You crack your sticky, dry lips open. "Can someone help me up please?"

Silence.

Your voice cracks. "Please?" You lift your head a little, gazing at the men in front of you. Their mouths are slightly ajar, blending into the surrounding darkness while their eyes sparkle.

"Please?"

They don't move at all. Some of them tear their eyes off you and rest their heads against their knees. But not a single person helps you. Your vision begins to blur. A tear drips down your face as you pull yourself toward a corner.

Your head touches a wall, your sore neck refusing to move even an inch.

Baba chuckles and pries your tiny fingers off his arm. "Alright, Yusuf. You have to go to sleep now."

"No," you whine. "I don't want to."

Baba glances toward his watch. "It's nine-thirty. Your brother has already gone to sleep."

You cross your arms. "Mahmoud is a baby. I'm a big boy."

"Oh, really? How old are you then, big boy?"

You hold out your fingers. "Six."

Baba laughs. "Even big boys have to sleep."

"You're big and you sleep late."

"Not that late." Baba wraps your legs in a blanket. "Now, you have to go to sleep, otherwise, you'll be cranky in the morning."

Baba reaches out for the light switch. "Baba," you squeak.

"Hm?"

"Can you tell me a story?"

Baba smiles, his beard crinkling as he does. He sits down next to you. "Hmm...have I told you the story of the chicken and the fox?"

You shake your head, squishing yourself into his side. He wraps an arm around you.

"Once upon a time, there was a chicken that laid ten eggs. She would sit on them every day, keeping them warm and talking to them. She couldn't wait until they hatched.

"But an evil fox was hungry and he saw the chicken in her nest. He licked his lips when he saw her eggs. 'I can eat all of those in one sitting,' he told himself. So he hid behind a bush and waited and waited for the mother chicken to go to the bathroom.

"And she did. She got up in the evening, gently petted her eggs and walked toward her coop. The fox jumped out from behind the bush and ran toward the nest. He clasped his hands together, thinking of all the dishes he could make from the eggs.

"But just as the fox was about to grab one of the eggs, the mother chicken came out of the coop. She smiled at him and asked the fox if he was hungry. The fox was in shock and nodded. 'Good,' said the chicken, 'I was just about to make dinner. Would you like to join me?'

"The fox looked from the eggs to the mother chicken and nodded. He followed her inside and wham, the mother chicken hit him with a frying pan.

'Don't touch my babies,' she shrieked. The fox jumped up and ran into the forest as the chicken kept waving the frying pain and screaming. Just then, the mother heard a crack from her nest. She ran toward it and saw that her chicks had hatched. She began hugging her children and the fox never came near her coop again. The end."

Your eyelids are now fluttering shut and a heaviness has settled on you. "Baba? Will you hit a fox with a frying pan if it tries to eat me or Mahmoud?"

Baba stands up and runs his hand in your hand. "Of course. I would chase it until it fell off the ends of the Earth. I'll make sure it never tries to eat you both."

He flips the light switch.

You jerk awake, pain shooting through your limbs as your muscles contract. Your lungs beg for air but it hurts to breathe. Everything hurts.

Your eyes flicker to the cell door. The walls around you begin to creep closer and closer but your body is frozen in place.

You can almost feel the gust of wind as a soldier coils his leg. You can almost feel the boots against your skin. You can almost taste the blood in your mouth.

"Turn the lights on. Turn the lights on. *Turn them on,*" you scream.

You try to pull yourself off the floor. The other prisoners are stirring awake now. You begin to sob. "Please, turn them on. Don't leave me in the dark. Don't leave me here."

But the lights never turn on.

laila

AMIR CRUMPLES ON his bed as soon as the door throws itself open. I step into the boiling air, the sun's rays hiding behind the house's walls. The hill of glass shards are still piled in the corner, sunlight from the torn plastic sheet above lighting them on fire. I slump onto a chair and hug its back. Amir's chest now rises and falls rhythmically.

My eyes remain glued to the cracked open bathroom door. The pipes hidden in the walls groan with each gust of warm air. The ceiling sags a little more than before, the walls bent close.

I glance toward the door and then back at Amir. The air around me begins to grow thick and sticky, clogging my lungs. I muffle my coughs and sprint outside, my hand wrapped around my throat.

The sun has climbed higher now. I shield my eyes, sight trained on the narrow street in front of me. The door *clicks* shut behind me.

I lie on my bed, tucked tightly in a blanket. I rub the bandage coiled around over the stub. Baba squats in front of me. "How are you feeling?"

I turn to the opposite direction, facing the wall. "Hm."

Baba sighs. "I know you're mad at me but I had to hold you down. Would you have liked for the doctor to accidentally cut your ear off because you moved?"

"Hm."

"At least tell me what you want to eat," he says, anguish laced in his voice.

A sandwich," I whisper.

Baba leans forward. "What?"

"I want a sandwich." I pause for a second. "And orange juice."

Baba grunts as he stands up. "Okay. I'll go buy some juice for you and when I come back, I'll make a sandwich. Can you take care of your little brother while I'm gone?"

I nod, still focused on the wall. The second the door closes, Amir begins to wail. I throw my blanket to the side and run down the hallway. I enter his room, watching as the baby inside screams and cries. I climb onto the mattress. "It's okay Amir. I'm right here."

His wails quiet down a bit as he looks at me. He opens his mouth. "Eh?"

"It's me, Laila. Look at this." I hold my hand out. The bandage coating the stump is now saturated with red. "They had to cut my finger off."

Amir's face crumples again, a sob at the edge of his tongue.

"It's okay. It hurt a lot but now, I'm a princess. I don't have to do anything. Baba is going to buy juice for me."

I clap my hands. Amir cocks his head to the side. I waggle a finger in front of his face. "No, you can't have any. It's all for me. You didn't have someone cut your finger off."

A shadow crosses in the cement in front of me, reaching my feet. I lift my head. An old man, in his late-seventies or so, grins at me. I force a smile to spread across my face.

"Nuh-uh-uh, that's not a genuine smile. You think you can fool an old man that easily? It's better not to smile than to pretend." He leans forward. "No one likes a liar."

"I'm sorry," I croak.

"Don't be sorry. Just remember my words. Now what are you doing? Are you lost, young lady?"

I shake my head.

"Are you sure? You've passed by my house three times."

"Oh," I mutter.

"Is everything alright?"

I nod, my eyes catching the potato in his hands. He looks toward his hand and then back at me. "Here, have it."

I take a step backward "No, no. It's fine."

He shrugs his shoulders and holds it out. "I'm not hungry right now and I have some bread inside. You look like you need it more."

I hesitate, my stomach lurching toward the vegetable. It's food. Fresh, free food.

"A-Are you sure?"

He nods, still smiling warmly. I reach out, my hands sinking a bit as the warmth from the potato seeps into my skin. I bob my head. "Thank you."

He beams. "Of course. If you're ever hungry again, come by with your family. I'd love to have guests."

My vision blurs from the edges, growing heavy. "Thank you. Thank you so much."

"My pleasure."

I spin on my heels and dash toward our home, making sure the potato is cradled to my chest. I throw open the door. Amir is a seated mass in the corner with his legs pulled to his chest. "Where did you go?" he mutters.

"That doesn't matter." I hold the potato in front of me. His eyes jerk open, darting from my face to the food in my hand.

"Can I hold it?" he asks.

I nod and he swaddles the vegetable. Within two seconds, the whole thing is gone. My head snaps forward and my jaw drops.

"That-that was for both of us," I cry.

He looks down. "Sorry, I was excited."

My stomach shrieks as I slump against a wall, crossing my arms over my chest. Tears threaten to break free from my eyes.

"I'm sorry," Amir mutters. He slaps a hand over his mouth to muffle his burp.

samira

DOTS CLOUD MY vision. I grip my head, nails digging into my hijab. The other women stare with knitted eyebrows. I shake my head, taking a step back.

"We can't go there. We can't," I mutter.

"Why? Where are we?" a sharp voice asks.

"That's ISIS," I whisper. "We need to go, now."

I take another shaky step backward, focused on the masked figure. His eyes lock onto mine. "Hey, where are you going?"

My vision begins to blur. Heavy boots *thud* closer. My muscles buzz and my feet take off.

"Hey. *Hey,*" the soldier calls out.

Thud. Thud. THUD. THUDTHUD.

Footsteps thunder behind me. With each second, the pounding gets louder and louder.

Crack.

A metal rod jams into my back, the air rushing out of my lungs. A boot rests on my ankle. I wrestle with it but it presses down.

"Running from the authorities? What are you guilty of?"

I suck in air through clenched teeth.

"Are you going to run again?"

I shake my head violently. The man presses harder, my bone screaming for freedom. "Don't worry. I'll make sure you never run again."

Crack.

A deafening sound escapes from my leg. I shriek with the surging pain and I curl into myself. The soldier keeps his foot on my ankle. "Come here," he orders and three shadows descend onto my burning skin.

"Where were you going?" the man growls.

"We were just trying to enter the city. Nothing else," one of the women says.

"Nothing else, huh? Well then, why would a group of women like you be out in the desert? That's not a normal sight. Do you have male relatives here?"

Someone nods. The man tilts his head. "What's his name?"

"Asad...Asad Khan," the woman responds.

"You don't sound so sure about that. How are you uncertain about your family's name?"

"I haven't met my brother in a long time. We've gone through a lot in the past couple of months. The name slipped my mind."

The soldier relaxes his foot but it's just a tiny relief. "And what things might that be?"

"We were in a detention camp," a girl pipes. The man's eyes snap toward her and they're narrowed.

"Detention camp? An SDF camp?" The man rests his hand on his rifle. "What scheme are you all part of?"

"Scheme? There's no scheme."

The soldier points his gun at the girl. "There's no point in lying. Lying is a sin and do you know where lying takes you? Jahannam."

"But I'm not lying. They just dropped us off in the middle of the desert without a single word."

The man scoffs. "I don't know what kind of an idiot you take me for. The SDF never lets anyone go. They've sent you all here with some sort of plan. Now, you four could be useful. Come with me."

.   .   .

I lean on one of the girls, gripping onto her arm with white knuckles. My foot drags behind me.

leaving a trail in the dirt. Beads of sweat drip into my shirt. A tattered building creeps closer and closer with every step. A thick lock hangs from the front door while black cloth barricades the windows.

"Inside," the soldier commands.

As soon as I step inside, I clamp a hand to my mouth. The air is stale with sewage while the floor is plastered with shredded clothes, soggy newspapers and plastic bags. A sliver of light sprays onto the walls, illuminating the women rocking back and forth in the corner. Their entire bodies and faces are draped in black burqas. Vomit floods into my mouth but I force it down.

The soldier rests his rifle on my shoulder. "I wouldn't think about running again. There are four guards stationed around the masjid with orders to fire."

"We can't get out?" a woman asks.

The soldier turns to her. "You can. All you need to do is get married."

My pulse rings in my ears. "I-Wh-What?" I sputter.

"You. Need. To. Get. Married. Otherwise, you're not leaving."

"But-"

Crack.

"Shut up."

A bolt of lightning strikes against my face. My cheek stings, the pain swelling until it's the size of a basketball. Everyone takes a step back.

"You're a feisty one. We'll just have to teach you some manners. You're lucky we take you sinners in and give you a chance to redeem yourselves. You modern women are too liberal, walking in the streets without covering yourselves properly. What a disgrace to your fathers, brothers and husbands. And all this talking back. A woman should be obedient. You were made from our ribs and in order to pay back that favor, you need to keep your mouths shut. Get rid of this American nonsense they've deluded you with. Once we conquer Syria, you'll understand."

The soldier turns and slams the door behind him, darkness embracing you all over again.

yusuf

YOUR EYES ARE still wide awake when they come back in the morning. You're taken to the same room and cuffed to the same chair. You keep your gaze fixed on the same crack on the wall. It trails down through the same splotch of purple, to the bare feet of the same corpse. The world grows fuzzy from the edges, taunting you. The commander emerges from the shadows.

"Did you sleep well last night?" he asks, his eyes scanning yours. "You look like a mess, you know? It's like someone painted you." He circles you. "You're red...and purple...and blue...and black."

He leans down. "Who did this to you? Tell me and I'll have them arrested. We can't have these monsters roaming the streets, can we?"

Your eyes remain glued to the spot. "Oh, you won't tell me. Was it that scary? I'm so sorry."

A lump grows in your throat.

"You know, all this can end if you answer me truthfully. I don't know why you have to make this so difficult for yourself. What did ISIS tell you to do?"

The commander jerks your head down to the bodies slumped near your feet. A sea of blood has sprung, coating the chair, the walls and the soldier's boots. "You don't want this to happen again, do you? Especially to you."

Your tongue is heavy and your throat is raw from screaming. The commander lets go of your chin, letting your head hang limply.

A hand slaps over your face, jerking it backward. A thick, white cloth blinds you, taking over every inch of your vision. Your mouth pulls open to inhale but as soon as your lips part, a wave floods into it. A wave of ice cold water. You try to straighten your head but it's forced back down. The water keeps coming and coming, filling your throat. Your lungs burn and beg to breathe.

But it doesn't stop.

And then it does.

Two hands clasp onto your shoulder. "Are you willing to crack?"

"I already told you," you croak.

"Not yet, I see."

Something grips on to your hair, pulling your head back again. The water is scalding now, the steam blocking your nose. The water seeps into your shirt and you can almost hear the sizzle of your skin.

You cough but the water keeps pouring into your throat and nose, refusing to stop. Your vision goes black from the edges and your soul claws up from the depths of your stomach, forcing itself out of your mouth.

"Don't kill him. If it was that simple, I would have done it ages ago. We need his confession to know what ISIS is targeting."

You gulp air greedily as soon as the hand releases your hair. The sides of your neck are on fire and you double over, water dripping down the side of your mouth as you cough.

Someone pats your back. "Now, now. It's not like I want to do this to you. We're doing this for our country. Don't you want a warless Syria, a country where the children can play freely? Don't you want all those refugees to come back and live peacefully? But to do that, we have to protect our land. You know something. I know you do. Come on, tell me. What do they want? What did they tell you?"

"I don't know," you whisper.

The hand forces your head back again. Through the soaking cloth, you can make out the silhouette of a face peering at you. Its warm breath tickles your skin.

"Do you know how many times I've heard that lie? So many times, I've lost count. It comes out of *every* mouth during *every* interrogation. But soon, they crack. They *always* crack."

He slams a fist against the chair. The force sends vibrations down your legs. *"Everytime.* Do you hear me? I'm no idiot to believe you just because you keep denying everything. You have one last chance."

"I—" You start but as soon as your mouth opens, the water comes back again. You thrash against the hand holding you back but with one tug, you're subdued. You twist your wrists but the metal holding you down bites deeper. You try to kick your feet but all they do is clink against the cuffs.

Your muscle begins to go limp with exhaustion. The steam begins to infect your blood, slowly taking over. And then, everything goes black.

laila

I REST MY head against the wall, staring at the sagging ceiling above. Amir's head is near my arm, fingers stroking my skin. "I'm really sorry, Laila," he murmurs.

"It's okay," I respond but my stomach shrieks in rebellion.

"Maybe there's some money here somewhere. Money Baba hid because he knew he was going to leave. When we find it, I'll buy you two potatoes with my share of the money."

I shake my head. "There's no money, Amir. There's nothing."

He sits up, his blanket crumpling to his feet. "Baba must have left something. It's not possible that he...abandoned us like that. He's hidden something here for us. I know it."

Just like you knew that Baba was in a neighboring town? I bite my tongue before the words can spill out. Amir stands up. "I'm going to check the walls for any hidden compartments. You can go check the back. Call me if you find something."

He skips toward the bathroom. I pull myself off the ground. The trap of hope. It caught Amir too. But the joy in his voice is enough for me to try.

Click.

The back door's lock snaps open, the wood sliding to the side. Four barrels stand erect to the right, the chewed out holes in their brown frames showcasing the emptiness inside. A couple of wood planks tilt toward them. The other side of the little yard is barren. I run my hands along the deep, aged scratches of the fence.

I stare at the girl zooming past me in her blue-and-green streaked bike. Its base is a shiny black, basking in the sunlight. My head turns an entire three-sixty, my eyes refusing to break from the bright colors.

"What are you looking at?"

Baba's fingers squeeze mine and my head jerks back. "Hm?"

Mama chuckles. "He asked what you were looking at with such awe. You haven't even looked at your own mother like that."

I shake my head. "Nothing."

"Come on. Let's go back home then," Baba declares. We turn back around. My eyes scan the area for the girl with the bike but only the tinkle of her bell is faintly carried by the breeze now. Mama's eyes linger on me but break when we arrive home.

"I'm going to put Amir to sleep now," she announces.

Baba nods and then turns toward me. "Time for you to get into bed too."

The next morning, my eyes catch a white blob near the edges of my vision. I reach for it, bringing the ink letters closer to my face.

Wake up.

I shoot straight off the bed, fingers curled around the strip of paper. On the ground, near my feet lies another. I pick it up.

Go toward your door.

The icy tile squeaks as my feet slide against it. I tilt my head to read the note taped onto my door. Open the door.

I turn the knob and peek through the crack, eyes landing on another paper fluttering against a wall. I step toward it. Walk toward the back door.

I tiptoe forward. Now open it.

I step outside, eyes settling on a glimmering pink bike. My eyes widen and a shriek erupts from my throat. I dash toward it. My fingers comb the glittering streamers on the handlebars and caress the tight leather seat. The word 'Laila' is painted across the frame in silver.

Chuckles ring in my ears. I spin backward to find Mama and Baba hugging the door frame, their faces glowing in the sunlight. I run toward them with my arms wide open. "Thankyouthankyouthankyou."

Four sets of hands rub my back. "We know how long you've been staring at those kids riding their bikes through the streets. We've been waiting for the perfect moment to give you this," Baba says.

"And this is the perfect moment," Mama pipes.

I rub my face against their legs, savoring their warm scent of cinnamon and lemongrass. "I love you," I mutter.

"We love you too."

"Did you find anything?' Amir calls out from inside. Wooden threads from the fence poke at my fingers.

"No," I shout back.

"I haven't either. Let's check somewhere else."

"Amir, there's nothing, okay? Baba hasn't left anything for us." Silence on the other end. There's nothing hidden, no money, no secret message, no nothing. It's just hope deluding a boy into thinking that there's something out there.

I gaze up at the murky sky, glaring at the stars that refuse to do anything but watch.

samira

I SHRIVEL INTO the corner, hand pressed against my throbbing ankle. The skin around it is jagged along my bone, pieces jutting out. When my fingers brush against them, a surge of pain ripples through my leg.

The walls inch closer, the faint glow of sunlight barely lighting up the cobwebs hanging in the corners. Every few seconds, a black dot zips across the room, finding a weak arm or a leg to feed on. The plastic bags on the ground crinkle with every slight movement, the tiniest reminder of life.

The door to the masjid swings open, light flooding into the room. "Everyone outside."

The soldier's eyes fall on me. "No one gave her a burqa?"

An indistinct voice responds and a black mass is shoved into the soldier's arms. He grumbles before turning toward me. "You, put this on."

He tosses the pile toward me. I stretch it out. "It—"

The soldier whips backward, his hand jerking toward his pistol. "Did you say something?"

I swallow the rock in my throat. "No"

He huffs. "Don't even think about coming outside without that on."

I slip my arms through the heavy cloak and force my head through the hijab piece. My knees bend with the weight, the ground taunting me with every step. I trudge toward the door, dragging my right leg behind me. The cloth of the burqa absorbs all the sun's heat as soon as I step outside. From the inside, it's dotted with yellow stains of sweat, only visible because of the little light entering the two slits cut for my eyes.

The soldiers force us into a line, our backs resting against the masjid's exterior. Men are gathered near the guards like a swarm of bees. They clamor over each other, their *bzz* ringing in my ears. The soldiers nod toward each other.

"You can come," one of them declares and the swarm descends, pushing each other to the ground as if it's a race.

I dig my foot into the dirt. The men all look the same with hollow cheeks and prominent glassy eyes. Their beards are half-shaven, patches of black, brown and gray all over their faces. Scars coat their entire bodies.

One of them, with small, brown eyes, snaps his head toward me. His arm is wrapped in a bandage, resting in a sling. As he approaches, the smell of sweat and garlic reeks from him.

"This one. I want this one," he announces. The soldier near me nods. The man grins. "Let's go."

My head begins to throb. Zayd's face flashes before my eyes: his radiant smile, his soft voice, his loving eyes. My vision begins to grow fuzzy from the edges.

The man turns around, his forehead wrinkling. He reaches for my wrist but I pull it back, my burqa ruffling in the breeze. I shake my head.

A soldier towers over me. "You don't want to make this hard on yourself. Believe me, you don't."

My eyes dart from the soldier to the "husband" and back. "I'm not going with you," I whisper.

The "husband" scowls and throws his hands in the air. "Nevermind. She's too rebellious. I can't have my wife disobeying me."

The soldier's eyes follow the "husband" as he returns to the line of women. Then, they snap toward me. His hand lunges behind my head, gripping onto the clump of hair inside the burqa. Each strand tears at my skull, a fire igniting inside my head. I claw at his fingers but he pulls harder.

The soldier rips the masjid door open and shoves me inside. "It seems like you haven't been here long enough. A little while longer, and you'll be begging men to marry you."

Slam.

The entire building trembles, a heavy stream of dust raining from the corners. I slide my hand inside the burqa and touch the raw patch of skin on my head. Strands of hair weave themselves in my fingers. When I pull my hand out, a thick clump of hair sticks to it.

My ears begin to ring. I can't leave. I'll have to marry someone. I'll have to marry someone other than Zayd. And Zayd's dead. My brother is dead. My entire family is dead. Yusuf is gone. I promised to care for him. I promised to protect him. I promised to keep him alive. But I'm stuck here. I'm stuck here until I get married. Then, I'll never find Yusuf. I'll never be allowed to go outside. I'll never find Yusuf. I'll never find him.

A sharp pain wracks my body and my left arm throbs. My chest constricts, my ribs cracking with the pressure. My fingers wrestle the burqa for my pocket but it's not here. I pat my sides, listening for the *clink* of metal.

But it's silent.

My mind flashes to when they went through my pockets. When they pulled it out. My inhaler.

yusuf

"ANOTHER DAY, NO results," the commander sighs. Your eyes are heavy while your throat is stripped dry. Patches of red, raw skin coat your entire body, the hot air stinging them.

"I'm hungry," one of the guards whines.

"Alright. Let's go eat," the commander says.

The acid in your stomach burns through the rest of your organs. "Can I have something to eat too?" you croak.

The commander scoffs. "Who do you think you are? A king? You're a *prisoner*."

Hunger ripples through your limbs. "Please?"

The commander rubs his face. "I can't deal with you right now." He gestures toward his minions. "Let's go."

The door clicks in place behind them. The singular lightbulb in the room caresses your face with its gentle halo. In the corner, three figures lay on the ground like paralyzed dancers.

You crawl toward the door, fingers latching onto the handle. You pull it down and push the metal block but it responds with a hushed *creak*.

Your arms burn with exhaustion now and you slide onto the floor. Your feet land into a puddle with a *splash* and the blood begins to climb up your skin, droplets spraying onto your face. I stare at the long red streaks on the walls, remnants of the last thing victims did.

The last thing they did because of you.

You didn't spin a good enough lie. You came up with a bizarre story. You didn't know the details.

And they died for it.

They died while you still breathe.

You look up toward the ceiling with its brown stains. "Ya Rabb, why? Why do I keep making these mistakes? Why do I keep costing people their lives?"

Your voice cracks. "O Allah, why didn't you strike me with lightning when I said those things to

Mama and Baba? Why didn't you let the bomb fall on me after I was rude to Mahmoud the last time I saw him? Why didn't you make me fall down the stairs or let the roof collapse on me when Aunt Samira had to leave Raqqa because of me? Why didn't you let a snake swallow me whole while I pushed her away? Why didn't you let that soldier break my neck after I made her cry in the van? Why didn't you let the commander shoot a bullet through my head after those people died for me?"

You sob into your hands. "Why? Why should I live?"

"Please live. I just want you to live."

"No. *No*," you shriek. "No, I don't want to live." You lean on your knees and pound on the door. "Just kill me right now. I won't tell you anything. Do us both a favor and shoot me. Make it slow if you want to. I don't care how you do it. Just end me right now. Make all this end."

Bang. Bang. Bang.

"KILL ME." You slump to the ground, tears bounces off the floor. Your breath hitches. "Please kill me. Please. Please."

laila

A GUST OF cold wind tickles my feet. My eyes crack open to the empty bed beside me. "Amir?" I call out.

The wind responds. I glance toward the creaking front door. Rays of white moonlight illuminate the pebbles just inches away from the tiled floor of the house.

I step outside. "Amir?" I call.

"Laila?" He responds, his voice past the front door. I peek out from behind the wall, eyes catching on the barren street.

"Boo." I flinch, stumbling backward. Amir grips his stomach as he bursts out laughing, his back resting against the left wall of the house.

I clench my teeth. "What are you doing in the middle of the night?"

"Is it a crime to have some fun?"

"In the middle of the night, yes. What if a soldier shoots you because he thought you were a spy?"

Amir sighs. "Oh, my dear. You still haven't learned, have you?"

I cock my head to the side. Amir's skin melts, brown pouring into his irises and his face widening just a bit. His nose shrinks while his mouth curls into a smile.

"Remember me?" Mama asks.

"Ma-Ma-Mama?"

She smiles. She opens her arms. "Come here."

I take a slow step forward. "Afraid of your own mother now, huh?"

"I would never be afraid of you."

She digs her nails into my arms. "Are you sure? Didn't you say you could get shot at night?"

"But that's differen—"

"How? How is it different? Let's say you take a step backward right now and a landline explodes."

My lungs collapse.

"Afraid now?"

I shake my head. Mama's pupils narrow. "You should be. You should be afraid of me after what you did."

"That's not my—"

"And now you're lying to yourself? I should have raised you better."

My fingers curl around my pants. Tears threaten to break.

Mama smiles. "So you do know it's your fault, then? Ahmed might still be here if I was alive. Amir would have had a mother to take care of him, instead of *you.*"

I take a step back.

"Uh-uh-uh, I wouldn't do that if I were you. There's a landmine. You wouldn't want your body blown into pieces, would you?"

I take another step backward. "You're not Mama."

She smirks. "Who said? People change. But you wouldn't know that. Not after begging me to play with you. That's why I'm dead."

I shake my head. "No, no, no."

Mama takes a step forward. "It's only fair for you to suffer the same fate, wouldn't you agree?"

Her grip on my arm tightens.

"No, please. It was an accident."

"Accidents have consequences."

My pulse rings in my ears. "I'm sorry, Mama. I'm sorry," I whimper.

She clicks her tongue. "Sorry isn't enough."

A shriek tears from my throat. I shoot straight up. Amir jolts nearby. "What's wrong, Laila? What's wrong?"

"No, no. Stay away from me. Stay away," I croak. I hold my arms in front of me, pushing him back.

Amir lurches forward and wraps me in a hug. "It was just a dream. Repeat after me. A dream."

"A dream," I repeat.

"Good, again."

"A dream."

PART III

samira

MY AIRWAYS BEGIN to tighten while my legs are almost floating, the numbness creeping up my bones. My eyes are frozen in place, locked on the ceiling. It sags from the center, thin cracks running across it. A swarm of flies rests on every surface possible. Their purple eyes glimmer in the little sunlight that escapes the boarded windows.

"Assalam Alaykum. Assalam Alaykum," Zayd *mutters as he turns his head to the right and then the left. He cups his hands together and bows his head, his lips moving slowly. I cross my legs and close my eyes.*

A couple of minutes later, he raises his head and nods toward me. I mutter my last dua and reach out to his face.

"Look," I say, "it's a gray hair." I gasp and chuckle. "You're getting old."

He laughs, his eyes closing as he does. "Oh no, what will I do?" He rests his head on my shoulder. "Don't worry. You'll be just as beautiful when you're old," he whispers.

I smile and rest my head on his.

"You know, they say that after you die, your mind plays its most beautiful memories for seven minutes." Zayd rubs his chin. "When I die, I'll first remember my dad, my mom, my two brothers, my cousins, my grandma, my aunts, my uncles...hmmm, I don't think I'm missing anyone."

I push his head off my shoulder. "Me, silly."

His eyes light up. "Oh, yeah. How can I forget my wife, the joy of my life?"

A smile tugs on my lips and I try to lift my fingers but the numbness has conquered them.

"Samira, Samira. At school today, the teacher asked us what we wanted to be when we grow up. You know what I said?"

I put my doll down and crawl toward my brother, shaking my head. He grins. "I want to be an astronaut."

I gasp with admiration. "So you want to go to the moon."

He shakes his head. "Not just the moon. I want to go to every planet in space and every time I come back, I'll bring you a rock from there. You'll be the only person to have them. And then, when the company pays me a million dollars, I'll buy a mansion for me and you. It'll have a swimming pool and slides so we never have to climb the stairs. And we can have a million cats as pets and eat chocolate cake every single day."

"Can we have dolphins in the pool?"

He taps his face. "Why not?"

"And we'll have a lot of toys?"

He smiles. "We'll have all the toys and candy in the world."

I giggle with excitement. "Really?"

He nods and I jump into his lap. He yelps in pain. "Don't kill me before then with your monkey jumps."

"Oops." I blow on his leg. "Is it better now?"

He nods. "All better."

My throat begins to close.

"No, no," Yusuf cries. His arms and legs are wrapped around his mother's waist.

"Come on Yusuf. It's just water."

"But what if sharks eat me?"

His mothers sighs. "There are no sharks here."

I wade into the water, my dress pooling around my ankles. "Yusuf, look. I'm in the water and I'm fine."

He turns his head toward me with glimmering eyes. "Do you see any sharks?"

"No, I don't see any near here." I run my hands against the ocean's surface. "The water is so cold and refreshing. You don't want to miss out, do you?" He shakes his head. "Then get off your mom and come here."

Yusuf turns to his mother and she nods. He climbs off her and waddles in the sand toward me. His tiny hands latch onto mine. He puts one foot inside the water, a smile spreading on his chubby face.

"See, it feels good, doesn't it?"

He nods eagerly and sits down. "It's cold," he shrieks.

"The cold is great. Watch, when you step out of the water, you'll start sweating like a volcano."

Yusuf reaches into the aqua water and pulls something out. He runs his fingers against the long, blueish-green plant. He holds it up. "What's this?"

I bend down. "Seagrass."

"What's that?"

"It's like the grass on land but in the water. It protects the little animals in the ocean from bigger fish."

He gasps. "Even sharks?"

I nod. "Even sharks."

He cocks his head. "But what about us?"

I raise an eyebrow. "What do you mean?"

"Does it protect us?"

I tap my chin. "It could if only it was alive."

Just then, a wave claws for the strand and it fades into the water, its vibrant green melting into the blue of the ocean.

I clench my heart, which is collapsing in on itself. My vision blurs and something drips down my face. I try to turn my head but my neck is stiff. My lungs burn and raspy noises erupt from my mouth.

A smile twitches on my face. "O Allah," I whisper with a heavy tongue, "protect Yusuf from the soldiers and all the harm that plagues this country. He has no one left but You. Please protect him. Please protect him."

The words start to die in my mouth and the edges of my vision grow dark. My lips move ever so slightly to utter the shahadah when my chest implodes, right after a smile blossoms on my face.

yusuf

THE DOOR SWINGS open. You flinch as the boots grow closer. "Have a restful night?" the commander asks.

You freeze.

"Aww, are you hungry?" He squeezes your cheeks and moves your head side to side. "Look, the poor boy's hungry. Bring him water."

Silence. "Are you serious?" one of the commander's minions asks.

"Yes, I'm serious."

The door opens and closes. The commander's fingers still dig into your face. A minute later, glass touches your lips. The cool liquid heals the fire inside your throat.

"Nuh-uh."

The glass pulls away from you. You barely crack open your unswollen eye.

"I can't give you something when you haven't given me anything. Now, to make things move a little *faster*, I have employed someone to help me. Someone very special to you. You see, I heard you were captured alongside your mother, isn't that correct?" The commander smiles slyly. "If you keep up this little game of yours, then let's just say, my finger may accidentally pull a trigger." He rests his hand on his gun. "Oops."

He cocks an eyebrow. "The choice is yours."

I know you'll never accept me as a mother but as your family, I want you to live.

I want you to live.

Live.

Live.

Live.

"As long as she lives," you croak.

The commander nods. "You have my word."

You shake your head. "That's not enough."

He smiles. "I swear to Allah that I'll set her free as long as you tell me the truth. Happy?"

You let your eyes fall to the ground, focusing on how the light ripples in the puddle of red near your feet.

"Now talk."

You shift against the wall, resting your shoulders on a corner. "It was a couple months ago. I was living with my-my mother and had to get bread one day. ISIS contacted me then. Said I was strong, healthy and would get paid if I did them a favor. Life is tough there. We barely get enough to eat and all the townspeople depend on the baker's kindness—"

"I don't care about all these meaningless details. What did they ask you to do?"

"They gave me a bomb and told me to deliver it to Huzajma."

"Who were they targeting with that bomb?"

"I don't know. I think I heard them saying it was supposed to target an SDF commander."

The commander leans toward you. "What was his name?"

"The target?"

He sighs. "The person who contacted you."

You shake your head. "I don't know. He never told me his name."

The commander's eyes dig through yours. "He must have had a code name, something. What did you call him?"

"Sir."

He cocks his head. "Sir? You called him sir?"

You nod. "And why was that?"

You lean your head backward. "I don't know. He said it was best for me not to know his name for my safety."

The commander scoffs. "Your safety, yeah right. Keep going."

"The bomb is hidden in the desert, near a tree with the word Allah carved into the trunk. I was going to go alone but my mother demanded that she come with me. She doesn't know the real reason I wanted to go. I told her that there was a job opportunity in Huzajma and that we would have enough to eat every day. But she didn't want to let me go alone. And then, you caught me."

A black shadow creeps over the puddle. The commander bends down and glares at you. "Anything else I should know?"

You meet his eyes and shake your head.

laila

THE SUN IS almost wide awake outside, its rays biting into my skin from the window. The sheet tied to the roof rustles. My stomach sinks toward the ground but its purring doesn't die down. I toss my blanket aside and trudge to the bathroom.

Tap. Tap.

"Yes?" I call out.

"Are you hungry?" Amir peeps.

I open the bathroom door to find him standing an inch away. His hair is disheveled and his eyes are droopy. "Are *you* hungry?" I ask.

"You didn't answer my question," Amir responds.

I shake my head. "I'm not."

Grrr.

I glance down at my trembling stomach. Amir's eyes narrow. "Why do you lie?"

I keep my gaze fixed on the floor.

"Why can't you just tell me the truth? How difficult is that? You don't have to protect me from anything. I'm thirteen, not four."

"Sorry," I whisper.

He grimaces. "I was thinking we could sell...Baba's mattress."

My head jerks up.

"I know you don't want to but it's the only thing we can sell for money. We need our mattresses and there's almost nothing else in the house that others would want to buy."

I nod. Amir's voice is quiet now. "But what if he comes back?"

I shake my head and squeeze his shoulders. "He's not coming back. He's not."

"Okay," Amir's voice cracks at the end. "Let's go then."

Amir coils a short rope around the middle of the mattress, forming a crevice in the thin foam. He heaves it onto his shoulders. I open my mouth. "I—I don't want to bother that old man again. I'm going to search the trash bins behind people's houses. Maybe I can find something there."

"No," Amir cries, "Don't go."

"It'll be better if we separate. More chances of finding food."

Light gushes through the crack in the door as Amir turns the doorknob. "I don't want to be alone. Please. I-I can't lose you too."

This is no time for emotions. We've barely eaten the past two days and if we don't find some way to get food, we'll die. shake my head. "I'll only be gone for a couple of hours. We'll meet back here before sunset, okay?"

"Will you be back on time?"

I nod. "Don't worry. I'll be back before you know it, in sha Allah."

.   .   .

I duck into an alley, allowing the darkness to swallow me whole. A green rectangular trash bin rests in the corner. I throw open the lid and bend over the edge. Slick, slimy liquid slithers up my arms. The stench of sewage and dead rats slaps my face while flies circle any piece of meat or fruit possible.

I huff, sealing the garbage world shut. A brown, thin liquid coats my fingers. I grimace and rub my hand against the lid.

The heat plays with my vision. My stomach is screaming again, surges of fatigue running through my limbs. I slump against a hospital wall and peer up toward the spotless sky. Something from the rooftop glints in the sunlight. I squint. On the edge of the hospital's roof is a yellow canister. Faded brownish spots dot the top while a hushed *hisssss* rings in my ears. A chemical smell tickles my nose.

I narrow my eyes, inhaling again. It's like the smell of a swimming pool mixed with disinfectant. My eyes begin to sting.

I dash into the streets.

"What's that smell?"

"Does anyone smell that?"

"What is that?"

"It smells like a chemical?"

"Did something leak from the hospital?"

BOOM.

yusuf

"CAN WE KILL him?" one of the minions jitters.

The commander straightens himself and smirks. "Sure."

A light blooms in the minion's eyes. He reaches into his belt, pulls out his pistol and rests a finger on the trigger. You look up at the gun's mouth. It's like a daydream, so mysterious yet alluring.

Click.

He steadies the gun and closes one eye. His finger begins to press.

"Wait," the commander booms.

Bang.

The minion flinches and his hand jerks to the left, the bullet barely missing my ear. He snaps his head toward the commander, wide-eyed.

"We don't want to make this *easy* for him. I'll let him suffer for just a bit longer. He's been an incredible burden on me. That seems fair, doesn't it?"

The blood drains from your face. "Please, just end me now."

The commander crouches down in front of you. He pinches your cheeks. "No."

He straightens himself, grunting as he does. "We'll leave him here. Let him rot for a bit before having some *real* fun tomorrow."

"*No. No,*" you shriek.

Thud.

The door slams shut, the murmur of the outside world dying with it.

laila

THE GROUND TOSSES me to the side, my head trembling with the impact. Debris rains from the sky and screams erupt from the streets. I pull myself off the dirt but a storm of feet slams into me.

I try to breathe but a wisp of chemical strips my throat raw. I clamp a hand over my mouth. "Amir," I call. "Amir."

People's hands, feet, arms and legs swarm in front of me, blurs of color blocking the street. "Amir," I cough.

I can barely hear my voice over the screams. Within seconds, people crumple to the ground, yellow clouds foaming out of their mouths. I tie the stray end of my hijab over my nose. "Amir."

I take a step forward with shaky legs. The dirt sways back and forth. My vision begins to blur from the edges. *"Amir,"* I cry.

"Laila," a distant voice calls out. I jerk toward the sound. "Amir. Amir."

An arm shoots out from the stampede. "I'm coming," I shriek.

Slam.

A woman carrying two children stumbles over me. My foot catches on her leg. "Out of my way," she hisses.

Shoes press onto my back. I yelp in pain, clawing at the dirt. My fingers brush against skin. I peer up to see a man groaning as foam drips from his mouth. His skin is yellow and his entire body is convulsing. I jerk backward.

My voice is sharp now. "Amir. *Amir. AmirAmirAmir."*

The screams are nothing compared to the deadly ringing in my ear. A hand grips my arm and tugs me. "Where are you going? The evacuation is this way."

I claw at the woman's fingers. *"Amir. Amir."*

The woman holds on. "He'll be where everyone else is. If you stay here, you'll die."

BOOM.

I tumble to the ground, wrapping my arms around my head. The smell gets stronger.

Crack.

A deafening sound echoes through the street. The screams, the cries, the wails, everything goes

Silent.

CRACK.

The pebbles on the ground begin to rumble. The building several feet away bends from the middle.

The screams start again.

And then, the building crumples to the ground like an old man whose cane was snatched from right under his fingers.

yusuf

YOUR BONES BEGIN to rumble, your head banging against the wall. You turn a bit, denying your curious eyes permission to open. The trembling grows stronger and stronger, your head slamming to the floor. A storm of dust pours down from the ceiling and then, *BOOM*.

A gust of wind knocks you backward. You throw your arms over your face and curl into yourself. A wave of debris slashes your skin while a cloud of dust infects your eyes.

Your fingers wrap around the faint clumps of hair left on your head. The ground begins to calm down and then, everything stops. You lift your head up ever so slightly, eyes searching the ashy air around you.

The wall in front of you lies as bricks on the floor. The metal door is bent from the middle while the knob is completely blown off. Next to your arms, a pile of gray shreds bite into your skin. You rub your eyes, the grains of ash sinking further into your swollen flesh.

Smoke begins to infect your lungs, coating them. You lay your head back down, staring at the gray above you. Your eye catches a hint of blue, chuckling at you.

You turn your head, watching a tiny, orange flame dance just a couple of inches away. A smile pulls on your lips and you reach out. Your finger sways in the fire and it begins to tingle.

A sign that you're still alive.

A sign that you're still alive even though you should be dead.

The smell of singed flesh tickles your nose and you pull your finger toward you. You gaze at the purplish-red flesh, at the tinge of black on the corners of your torn skin.

Krrr.

A slab of concrete begins to shift several meters away from you. A man pulls himself out from underneath and crawls away. Coughing begins to ring in the air while some of the other prisoners groan and whimper in pain.

Near your head, debris crunches as gentle footsteps creep toward you. A figure crouches.

"Are you alright?" it asks.

You keep your eyes fixed on the faint hint of blue and nod.

"You're hurt."

You wrap your fingers with your hand. "Come on. Let's get out of the smoke."

You sink further into the shattered tile floor. The elderly man beside you presses a hand to your shoulder. "It's best to get out as soon as possible before damage occurs. Smoke inhalation can kill you."

You shake your head just a little. The man grunts as he leans backward until he's sitting. "You can take some time, if that's what you want. I'll wait with you."

You flicker your eyes toward him, eyes tracing the red hole on his face. He smiles, a tender, sincere smile, right before falling limp to the side.

laila

THE WOMAN TEARS me off the ground, weaving in and out of the crowd. I try to wrench her fingers off but they bite deeper into my skin. "Let me go," I strain.

"No," she growls.

"Let go. Let go. *LetgoLetgoLetgo.*"

She pulls me forward and I stumble over someone's leg. In the corner, children hug their quivering parents, tears running down their faces. People crumple to the ground in coughing fits, foam dripping down their mouths. The smell eats at my lungs and my limbs get lighter and lighter.

I stagger down. The woman tugs me up. "Don't you dare."

My voice is hoarse, raw and stripped completely. "Amir," I croak.

The blurs around me begin to melt into the wind. My eyes are heavy now. Soon, the buildings vanish from sight, a sea of dirt flooding into view. My knees fold and I skid across the ground. "Amir. Amir."

Then everything goes black.

yusuf

CRUNCH. CRUNCH. CRUNCH.

Distant voices echo in the ash. "You all search there and there. We'll look here."

Footsteps creep closer, not caring to hide their tracks. "I found one," someone calls. A pained groan follows the voice.

"Get them outside. Extinguish any fire you see."

The ground near you begins to shift and then stops. A man, with deep wrinkles hanging from his cheeks, crouches down beside you. His head is wrapped in a bulky, white helmet.

"Can you walk?" he asks.

You shake your head. The man's gaze turns toward the elderly man beside you. He takes his glove off and presses his fingers against the corpse's neck.

"Gone," he whispers. He closes his eyes for a second, before turning back toward you.

"Alright. I'm a White Helmet and we're going to get you out of here. It might hurt a little but I'm going to have to carry you."

He slides his hands underneath you. You shift away from him and he cocks his head. "Is something wrong?"

"I'm staying," you croak.

"No, you're not." His hands reach out toward you.

You rub your back against the floor, your back stinging as shards tear your skin, shaking your head at the same time. The White Helmet lurches toward you. His iron hands pull you off the ground and over his shoulder.

Your leg screams as it dangles limply and a sharp pain shoots through your neck. "Let go. Let go," you shriek. The White Helmet takes a step forward. Your eyes catch on the stains of flesh blood from where you were lying down. You dig your fingers into his back. "I'm staying. I'm staying. *I'm staying.*"

You thrash your leg, the other one completely unresponsive. *"I'M STAYING."*

You ball your hands into fists and beat the White Helmet but he continues walking, not saying a single word as you continue to wail.

.   .   .

You lay on a bed, your sleeve cut open. A man in a white coat stands behind you, a constant sharp burning sensation surging through your shoulder. The doctor steps forward.

"I'm going to stitch up the wound. Unfortunately, it's deep so it won't heal well if I leave it. You'll feel some tingling but it shouldn't be too bad."

You keep your eyes fixed on the rippling cloth of the tent. A needle pricks your shoulder but you barely register the feeling.

.   .   .

Now, you're plopped in a chair. A doctor sits in front of you, his fingers woven together and his chin resting on the little platform they make.

"Do you have any family here?"

"My aunt," you whisper.

"Do you know where she is?"

You shake your head. "She was in the camp with me but I haven't seen her."

The doctor cocks an eyebrow. "There were no women there at all. Everyone we found were men."

Your head jerks up and your chest tightens. "She's not here?"

The man shakes his head. You grip onto the armrests of the chair. "Where is she?"

"I don't know."

Your fingers wrap tightly around the armrest, your knuckles turning white. *"Where is she?"*

The doctor's eyes lock with yours. "We don't know. I'll let the others know to keep a look out and maybe we'll find out where she is."

"She's dead, isn't she?" you mutter.

"Sorry?"

"She's dead, right?"

"No, no, she's not."

You lurch forward and dig your nails into the man's arms. "You're lying to me, aren't you?"

He shakes his head.

"You're lying. You're lying. *You're lying.*"

Your heart pounds against your ribs. The anger running through your veins takes hold of your muscles, disabling them.

"She's dead," you croak, your fingers slipping until they're limp.

The doctor squeezes your shoulder. "No, she's not. She wasn't in the building when the bombs were dropped. She's alive somewhere. But since we have no idea where she is, we're going to have to send you to Turkey with the others."

"I'm staying here."

The doctor sighs. "You can't. It's not safe."

"I can't leave her."

"We don't know where—"

"I can't," you interrupt.

The doctor shakes his head. "I'm sorry but I'm not asking you." You open your mouth but he holds a finger up. He gets up and exits the tent, your mouth hanging open.

laila

MY EYES FLUTTER open, a blank, white sky smiling at me. My hand hangs over the side of a mattress, caressing the ground. Something hard digs into my cheeks and blocks the edges of my vision. I run my hand over it, tapping the plastic. I inhale a gust of cool, pure air.

"You're awake?" A woman in blue asks. I nod ever so slightly.

"Alright. I'll get the doctor and she'll tell you if you're ready for your mask to be taken off."

I reach for her arm as she turns. She peers over her shoulder. "Amir," I croak.

She cocks her head. "Is Amir a family member?"

I nod. She smiles. "Alright then. I'll check around to see if he's here."

I release the nurse's skin and she turns a corner. My vision is a bit more steady now, the white above me ripening to shadows and wrinkles. Footsteps fade in and out of the tent, gentle murmuring ringing in my ears.

"Amir," I whisper.

Thud. Thud. Thud.

A hand rests on my forehead. My eyes dash to meet a woman in white, a stethoscope hanging from her neck. She's a little older, maybe in her early forties, with sunken eyes and deep bags underneath them. Her face is framed in a brown hijab, which sticks to the corners of her cheeks due to sweat. "What's your name, sweetie?"

"Laila."

"What a beautiful name. My younger sister is also named Laila." The metal disk of her stethoscope lands on my chest. "Inhale for me."

I take a deep breath, watching as my chest rises and then falls. The doctor nods and uncoils the mask off my face. The air is warm, tinged with sweat and medicine. "You're lucky the chemicals didn't kill you."

"Amir," I murmur.

The doctor leans in. "Sorry?"

I muster all my energy. "Amir."

She cocks her head. "No one told me about an Ami-" Just then, the nurse from earlier jogs over to the doctor and whispers something in her ears. I strain to listen. The doctor nods, waving her hand to dismiss the nurse.

"I'm sorry. We don't have anyone named Amir in any of the tents."

I shoot straight up, my head spinning as I do. "Oh—" the doctor begins.

"What did you say?" I cough.

"I'm sorry, Laila."

I shake my head. "No, he's here. He has to be." My voice grows louder, silencing all the others. "Where is he? Where is he?"

All eyes turn to me. The woman from earlier, who dragged me out of Douma, crouches in front of me. She runs her hands through my hair. "Shhh."

I jerk my head away. *You. Where is he?*

She shakes her head. "I don't know who you're talking about."

I rattle her shoulders. The doctor tries to pry my hands off her. "Now, now, no need to get violent."

Anger surges through my veins. *Where. Is. He?*

The woman shakes her head again. My hand flies straight across her face. Tears cloud my vision. "You took him from me. You killed him. *You killed him.*"

Nurses swarm around me but I kick, punch and scream. *"You took him. You took him. You took him."*

Something icy begins to course through my veins. "You...you...took...him."

Everything goes black.

yusuf

A VAN PULLS up to the tent. Volunteers with large boxes in their hands swarm toward it, throwing open the trunk. Some of them tear open the tops and lay cans, bottles and bandages out on the ground.

You keep your fingers curled around the armrest of the chair. Your knuckles are almost transparent now, the bones fading away.

A young man, whose helmet is still wrapped around his head, peeks through the opening in the tent. "Get ready. We're about to leave."

You force yourself off the chair and limp outside. Your feet tingle as they make contact with the sand while the sun bites into your face. You make no effort to block it.

You might as well let yourself fade into ashes.

laila

Several Years Later

THE WOMAN IN front of me peers over her glasses. "And why do you want to join the White Helmets, Laila?"

I gulp in air. "Your organization is something that should not exist."

The woman flinches and grips her pen. "Excuse me?"

"I mean, you don't want to have this organization that helps with bombings and chemical attacks to remain. That would mean the war would have to last forever."

The woman leans in, clasping her hands together. "Continue."

"I would like to join so I can bring an end to this organization, to make it a part of history."

I glance up from my clenched hands, at the woman's heavy eyes. "I really hope you are able to do that. I really do." She clears her throat. "You can start tomorrow. If you go down to the nurses' station, they can give you a uniform."

I nod, the intricate knot in my stomach untangling itself.

.   .   .

I pin my hijab to my uniform, thrashing to see if it moves. My heart starts to race. I push through the double doors, a waft of disinfectant and bandages running to my nose. My eyes run along the rows of patients: some wrapped in thick layers of bandages, some groaning in pain with fever, others with their eyes shut and sweat dripping down their glistening faces.

One, two, three, four, five, six...

The numbers dive into an abyss as my eyes land on the pale boy with curly, black hair. His spine protrudes through his hospital gown and his head tips back as he gulps a glass of water.

Thump. ThUMP. THUMP.

I step toward him, his pure, sea-green eyes beaming at mine.

AUTHOR'S NOTE

And the Seagrass Fades is a work of literary fiction but what the characters experience every day in the war-torn country of Syria is real.

Many people have heard about the Syrian Civil War. The conflict started in 2011 when a group of children and teenagers were caught doing graffiti, which was a crime. The kids were instantly arrested and tortured in prison. When their parents and other Syrians caught wind of this, they took to the streets with banners and other protest material.

Unfortunately, the president, Bashar Assad, took this as a threat to his power so he sent the military to take care of the problem. Their solution: shooting into the crowds.

That was just the start to the killing. Factions began to break off, each with different ideologies about the government. This was exactly what the Assad regime feared and this gave the president the justification he needed to start bombing and slaughtering his own people.

Among those factions is the Islamic State (ISIS). The extremist group traces its roots to Iraq and set its sights on the crippled country of Syria, with the goal of establishing a caliphate. Slowly, they began to conquer Syrian cities one by one, subjugating the citizens to horrific conditions. They drive men and boys into their armies under threats of death and torture while forcing women to stay behind closed doors. If a woman is found outside without a father, brother or husband, she is locked in a masjid with only one way of escape: marriage. Of course, those women have no choice in their marriage; they're sold off to the first person who wants them.

Another faction is the Syrian Democratic Forces (SDF). They are the rebel group the Assad government is trying to extinguish. Among one of their prominent activities are their internment centers. Anyone suspected of ISIS or Assad affiliation is sent to those buildings where they are tortured, starved and isolated for two reasons: confession or for entertainment. Countless witness testimonies give accounts of the gruesome conditions inside those centers. Bodies are left to rot, prisoners are beaten to the brink of death, people are violated, and so, so much more.

All these factions come together in an intricate web of conflict, with each group fighting the others. The SDF is trying to infiltrate the Assad government while pushing ISIS out (as of October 2024, they have captured a large portion of ISIS territory). The Assad regime is focused on the rebels, bombing cities of the map for suspected rebel presence.

What happened in Douma in 2018 was just as described. The Assad government suspected the city of housing rebels so in an effort to annihilate their enemy, they set off chemical bombs in the area. Traces of chlorine, dichloroacetic acid, trichloroacetic acid, chlorophenol, and other deadly chemicals were found on bodies, buildings and the air. The chemicals in the bombs, along with smoke and falling infrastructure, resulted in the deaths of 40 people and any number between 100 and 650 people were wounded.

It's been thirteen years since the start of the Syrian Civil War. Thirteen years of constant warfare, poverty and massacre. Countless people have lost their loved ones. Children sob in the streets due to hunger, their bones sticking out from underneath their skin. The elderly are paralyzed due to lack of nutrition. Bodies lay face down on the streets.

It's been years since this war has been forgotten. So I urge you, please, please, don't forget them. Don't forget the Syrian men, women, and children who are hoping for a day without bloodshed.

One voice can't change much but if we speak together, the whole world will listen.

Kian Sabik

To receive exclusive access to behind the scenes, sneak peeks and more, sign up for my newsletter:

I would really, really appreciate it if you could leave a review on Amazon & Goodreads for ATSF. Most people don't realize how much a couple sentences mean to an author. It means a loooooooooooooot.

ACKNOWLEDGMENTS

Did I say that EPOF was the most difficult novel to write?? I don't know what I was thinking. ATSF was definitely much, much, much harder to handle. They say that writing is a muscle that grows stronger with practice. When I first started on ATSF, that muscle was practically dead due to my one year hiatus. Thank you to:

Mom and Dad for supporting me throughout the whole process and helping me with every aspect.

My siblings for letting me bounce countless, silly ideas onto you both and for helping me with the small, tedious tasks of publishing.

My sister. Let's list everything you are: my editor, my map designer, my idea-giver. I'm definitely missing things. Thank you for sticking with me the entire journey of every single novel I've written.

Mr. Gillin. Thank you so much for everything you have ever done for me. You get the raw, unedited drafts of every book yet you still read them with patience and care. Both ATSF and I wouldn't be where we are without you. I'm eagerly waiting for your novel to come out one day. That might not happen in your eyes but I have hope.

My cover designer from Ebook Launch for designing this stunning cover. I was afraid that nothing would beat EPOF's cover but as soon as I set my eyes on this cover, I knew that that was just my anxiety speaking.

Everyone who has spread word about my novels, whether online or by mouth. You don't know how much it means to me.

And last but not least, you, the reader. You are why I write in the first place. I hope you resonate with the characters in *And the Seagrass Fades.* Please remember that the Syrian Civil War is not a tragedy but a story waiting for you to turn around.

Always remember, you are the difference.

ABOUT THE AUTHOR

Kian Sabik is a reader, author, student, and occasional procrastinator. She began writing at the ripe old age of twelve; and since pouring her first novel into the pages of a random composition book, she's never looked back. Through her writing, Kian hopes to illuminate the forgotten stories of others around the world, from both the past and the present. On the rare days she has free time, Kian spends her time reading, playing board games, learning Chinese, walking, and munching on chocolate (not for too long, though).

Want to connect with me?
- Follow me on Instagram: @kian.sabik
- Visit my website and subscribe to my newsletter at https://kiansabik.square.site/
- Follow me on Goodreads!